# SUZANNAH
# STRIKES GOLD

# SUZANNAH STRIKES GOLD

## ELAINE SCHULTE

ZondervanPublishingHouse
*Grand Rapids, Michigan*

*A Division of HarperCollinsPublishers*

Suzannah Strikes Gold
Copyright © 1992 by Elaine Schulte

Requests for information should be addressed to:
Zondervan Publishing House
Grand Rapids, Michigan 49530

**Library of Congress Cataloging-in-Publication Data**

Schulte, Elaine L.
   Suzannah strikes gold / Elaine L. Schulte
     p. cm. — (A Colton cousins adventure : bk. 3)
   Summary: In 1848, having survived the long, dangerous journey west,
twelve-year-old Suzannah and her cousin Daniel call on God's help to
face the temptations and the hardships of the California gold fields.
   ISBN 0-310-54611-7 (paper)
   [1. Frontier and pioneer life—Fiction. 2. Overland journeys to
the Pacific—Fiction. 3. Gold mines and mining—Fiction. 4. California
—Fiction. 5. Cousins—Fiction. 6. Christian life—Fiction.] I.
Title. II. Series: Schulte, Elaine L. Colton cousins adventure : bk. 3.
PZ7.S3867Sv  1992
[Fic]—dc20
                                                   92-10321
                                                             CIP
                                                               AC

*All characters are fictitious with the exception of Mose Schallenberger, who became snowbound
in the Sierra Nevada Mountains during a covered wagon trip to California in 1844.*

*Edited by Anne Severance*
*Interior design and illustrations by Louise Bauer*
*Cover design by Jack Foster*
*Cover illustration by Dan Johnson*

*Printed in the United States of America*

93  94  95  96  97 / DH / 10  9  8  7  6  5  4  3  2

*To the shining lights
on Del Obispo in San Juan Capistrano*

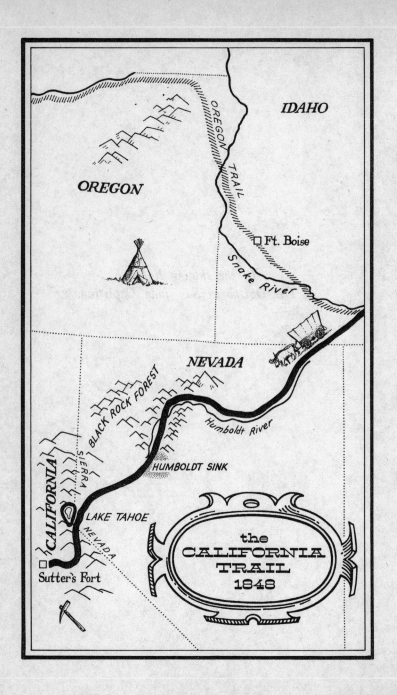

IDAHO

OREGON

OREGON TRAIL

☐ Ft. Boise

Snake River

NEVADA

BLACK ROCK FOREST

Humboldt River

HUMBOLDT SINK

SIERRA

CALIFORNIA

LAKE TAHOE

NEVADA

☐
Sutter's Fort

the
CALIFORNIA
TRAIL
1848

# CHAPTER ONE

California, here we come!"

Twelve-year-old Suzannah Colton could not contain her excitement this glorious August morning in 1848. She shouted again at the top of her lungs, "California, here we come!"

Her fellow travelers on the journey west took up the cheer as the long line of covered wagons rolled forward: "Californy, here we come!"

Walking along beside the wagon, Suzannah looked down at her red calico dress, new when they'd started out, and the moccasins she'd gotten from the Indians in a trade back on the prairie. They might be scuffed, and her dress faded from the hot sun and all those creek washings, but it didn't matter. Most of the time, travel by covered wagon was pure adventure. To think they'd come all the way from

Alexandria, Virginia, and now they were on their way to California!

Suzannah's sunbonnet dangled by its strings against her shoulders. *I'd better put up my bonnet before I'm told,* she thought. But its curved brim was like a horse's blinders, and when she wore it, she could only see straight in front of her. Besides, she liked the feel of her thick brown braids bouncing against her back. Still, with a grown sister and two aunts along, she knew she'd soon be hearing, "Put up your sunbonnet, Suzannah!"

Daniel, her thirteen-year-old cousin, cracked his whip over the heads of their six oxen. "Giddap, boys!" he yelled at them. "Giddap!"

The huge oxen plodded along a little faster, the covered wagon creaking behind them. Pauline, her older sister, sat in the driver's seat of the wagon, sketching the trees and the Raft River. Her little son, Jamie, was nowhere in sight. He's probably playing inside the wagon, on the dusty quilts in back, Suzannah guessed.

"I'm glad we're going to California, after all," she told Daniel as they walked alongside the oxen. "I'd like to find some of that gold myself."

Daniel kept a watchful eye on the oxen. "Me, too."

"Which?" Suzannah asked. "You're glad we're going to California? Or you want to strike gold?"

"Mostly glad we're going to California." Daniel grinned, his brown wavy hair rippling in the breeze.

"And I thought you were so set on going to Oregon, you and your itchy feet!"

"I was, at first," he replied. "I've always wanted to see the Oregon Territory ... ever since Father told me about meeting Meriwether Lewis, the great explorer. It's where we were headed when we left Missouri."

She thought back to a few days ago at Fort Hall,

when riders had brought news of a gold strike. "Gold in California!" they had called. "Gold the size of potatoes!"

"Is that the truth?" the wide-eyed emigrants had asked.

The riders showed them an article from *The Californian*, a San Francisco newspaper. It read: "The whole country, from San Francisco to Los Angeles and from the seashore to the base of the Sierra Nevada, resounds to the sordid cry of gold, gold!, GOLD! while the fields are left half planted, houses half built, and everything neglected but the manufacture of shovels and pickaxes."

"San Francisco is deserted!" the riders had exclaimed. "Everyone's gone out to the gold fields! The stores are closed . . . newspaper offices shut down . . . even the boats in the harbor look like ghost ships! It's the same in Sonoma, Benicia, San Jose . . . empty streets and loose cattle wandering through the grainfields!"

Before long, Suzannah's family and plenty of others who had set out for the Oregon Territory had changed their plans. Of the twenty-six wagons, eighteen were now bound for California. Reverend Benjamin had prayed for them before he left with the Oregon group, and there had been many tearful goodbyes as the wagon train split in two directions.

"Maybe all that gold will be gone by the time we get to California," Daniel mused.

"Well, that's a gloomy thought!"

"I was just wondering how Charles would feel if it's all gone before he gets there."

Suzannah darted a quick look at Pauline, who was still busily sketching and paying no attention to them. Her handsome husband, Charles, was a no-account fellow who gambled away everything he could get his hands on. In fact, he was the reason their plans had changed.

"I'm going to California—no matter what!" he had

said, and had ridden off with the miners, without a backward glance at his wife and child. That's when Uncle Franklin had suggested they all ought to go, mainly to keep the family together.

Daniel rolled his green eyes skyward. "I'm glad Charles isn't *my* family."

"Well, he's not mine by choice, either, and you know it, Daniel Meriwether Colton!" Suzannah answered. Pauline had married Charles right after their parents died, but instead of helping, he'd gambled away their house in Alexandria, Virginia, causing them to flee to Missouri. When that hadn't worked out, they'd headed for free land in Oregon. And now, California—

"If only we could be settled in a real house in a real town, like we were in Alexandria—" Suzannah sighed.

Daniel said, "If we don't like California, we can always go north to Oregon later, after we have enough gold to get settled."

She shrugged. "With Charles, you never know what'll happen next."

"The more I think about California," Daniel said, "the more I think I might like to find some of those potato-sized gold nuggets."

"I would, too. Think I'll get myself a wheelbarrow and just run along and scoop 'em up," Suzannah said.

Daniel gave her the famous Colton grin. Not just a smile tipping up the corners of his mouth, but a big wide grin that spread all the way up to the crinkles in his eyes. Daniel's grin always reminded her of Father, and of his brother, Uncle Franklin.

"Don't get your hopes up too high!" he warned. "There might be enough to fill a pocket or two, but not a wheelbarrow!"

"Still, even a little gold can come in mighty handy," she argued. "Remember the gold coins Father gave me?"

Reminded of her father, Suzannah thought of the picture of her parents that she carried on a hook in the covered wagon. In that picture, Mother's golden hair was pulled back into a neat bun at the back of her head. She looked just like Pauline, except Pauline's face was brown from the sun now, even though she always wore her sunbonnet.

As for Father . . . well, except for bangs across her forehead and long thick braids, Suzannah had been told she was the spittin' image of him—freckles, blue-green eyes, brown hair with a cowlick, and all.

Just thinking of Mother and Father and their brick house in Virginia made her eyes fill with tears as she walked along on the dusty trail.

"Courage," Father would have said.

And Mother's favorite Psalm came to mind: "Yea, though I walk through the valley of the shadow of death, I will fear no evil: for thou art with me."

In the beginning, they had traveled through prairies bright with wildflowers and broad passes through the Rocky Mountains. They had been blessed with water from the rivers they followed, and buffalo for meat. And even when they'd run out of trees for cookfire wood, there had been plenty of dried buffalo droppings for fuel.

But the hardest part of the journey—the part that most resembled "the valley of the shadow of death"—had been the desert. There Charles had had to shoot two of their dying oxen, Lily and Petunia. Now there were only Rose, Iris, Daisy, and Marigold, and two more they'd bought from the Murphys—Sweet Pea and Dandelion. All six of the oxen were lots thinner than when they had started.

From the front of the wagon train, someone shouted, "California, ho!" and others repeated, "California, ho!"

In front of them, Daniel's mother and father—Aunt

Ruthie and Uncle Franklin—walked together alongside their wagon. "California, ho!" they called, laughing.

*At least California's only two months away. That's better than four months to Oregon.* With that thought in mind, Suzannah let out her own "California, ho!"

At that, Pauline looked up from her sketchbook. "Suzannah Colton! Put up your sunbonnet, or your skin will dry up like old leather!"

"I knew I'd hear that sooner or later," Suzannah complained. Reluctantly she pulled up her bonnet.

"Daniel, tell me again what those California men said about how the gold was found."

"Only that someone was building a sawmill on the North Fork of the American River, and they found bits of gold in the mill's tailrace. You know, in the ditch."

"And then everyone started searching?"

He drew an impatient breath. "You already know the story. That's when they began to find the big nuggets."

"I just wanted to get it all straight in my head," she explained. "It's hard to believe until I can picture it."

At that moment Pauline called down from her perch, "Where's Jamie?"

"Isn't he in the wagon with you?" Suzannah asked uneasily about her two-year-old nephew.

"I thought he was with *you*—"

Suzannah's heart sank.

"Is Jamie in your wagon?" she called ahead to Aunt Ruthie.

Aunt Ruthie shook her sunbonneted head. "No, I haven't seen him. Don't tell me he's missing—"

"I hope not!" Suzannah replied. "Maybe Aunt Pearl—"

She hurried ahead to the first of her family's three wagons. Aunt Pearl's two collie dogs, Lad and Lass, greeted her with loud barks and wagging tails, but there was no time for them now. "Have you seen Jamie?" she asked her aunt and fifteen-year-old stepcousin Garth.

"Not since breakfast, dear," Aunt Pearl replied.

"Not me," Garth said sullenly, as if he were being accused of wrongdoing. "Likely stolen by Indians. But I ain't been near 'im."

"Didn't say you *had* been," Suzannah said, turning to run back again.

She thought of Garth's real mother, who had been killed by Indians some years ago while she was hanging out clothes. That accounted for his hatred of Indians. But did it also explain why he had been cold to everyone else for most of the trip? He had even been rude to Aunt Pearl, his new stepmother, and she was real easy to love.

Suzannah ran past Aunt Ruthie, who called out, "The last I saw of Jamie, he was playing peek-a-boo from the bushes back behind the campfire. I thought Pauline was going to get him, but—"

Just then, Captain Monroe rode down the line of wagons, his bushy brown beard catching the glint of sunlight. "What's wrong here?"

"Jamie . . . he's missing!" Suzannah told him. "I thought he was with Pauline, and she thought he was with me—" There was no sense in telling him that Pauline should have kept up with her own child.

"Halt the wagons! Halt the wagon train!" Captain Monroe bellowed.

Suzannah shouted to Daniel as she ran past. "I'm going back to the cookfire at our last camp! Aunt Pearl says he was hiding behind the bushes when she saw him last."

"I have to tend the oxen or I'd go with you—" Daniel began.

But Aunt Ruthie was already there. "You're faster, Daniel. I'll tend the oxen. You go help Suzannah and Pauline look for Jamie."

Daniel and Pauline quickly caught up, and Suzannah pulled back her sunbonnet so she could see all around.

"I don't know what's wrong with me!" Pauline wailed. "How could I have let Jamie get away?"

*Dazed*, Suzannah thought, *Pauline has been acting dazed.* But she didn't dare say it. Others in the wagon train sometimes seemed confused, too. And Pauline was probably worried about Charles.

Suzannah wasn't worried about Charles—she was just plain angry. The more she thought about Charles Herrington riding off to the gold fields without his wife and child, the madder she got.

"Don't worry, Pauline," Suzannah said, her anger giving her fresh courage. "We'll find Jamie. He couldn't have gotten far."

Pauline began to sob. "I heard wolves last night—"

"Don't think about that now," scolded Suzannah.

"What's the trouble?" asked others in the wagon train as the search party hurried by their wagons.

"Jamie's missing," Suzannah explained again and again. "Have you seen him?"

"Not since the last camp," one woman replied.

"Not since breakfast," another said.

"J-a-m-i-e! J-a-m-i-e!" Suzannah called, hoping to see him toddling along in the cloud of dust behind the last wagons. But there was no sign of him. He wasn't even in the rear with Ned Taylor, the older boy they'd hired in Missouri to tend the loose livestock.

"Haven't seen him at all today," Ned said.

"He must still be back at our last camp," Suzannah decided.

"If I'd only insisted on staying in Virginia, this wouldn't have happened!" Pauline cried. "I'll never forgive myself! What kind of a mother am I?"

"You're a good mother," Suzannah insisted. "Lots of

emigrants have been a little . . . upset lately. We've all been through a lot."

"What if Indians took him?" her sister wailed. "Captain Monroe said the Bannocks here are unfriendly. What if they kidnapped him?"

"Stop that!" Suzannah snapped, suddenly as scared as her sister. She knew they might have real trouble with the Bannocks. Just days ago Garth had almost shot an Indian girl who was picking berries in the woods. Fortunately, Daniel had stopped him in time.

Moments later, Uncle Franklin rode up on his horse. "I'll ride back to the campsite in case Jamie's still there."

"Wait!" Pauline cried. "Let me ride with you!" But when she tried to mount the horse, her knees buckled and she collapsed on the ground like a half-empty sack of flour.

"Pauline!" Suzannah grabbed her sister's shoulder and shook her. "Pauline, wake up!"

After a moment, Pauline opened her blue eyes wide, then looked around vaguely.

Behind them, Suzannah saw Captain Monroe with a search party of men on horseback. "Go on with them," Suzannah told Daniel and Uncle Franklin. "I'll stay here with Pauline."

She knelt on the ground, fanning her sister's white face as the men rode by, their horses' hooves kicking up clouds of dust. Daniel followed on foot, with Lad and Lass.

Pauline's voice quivered. "I can almost see his name on a grave marker like those back on the trail—*Jamie Herrington, aged 2 years, Rest in Peace*—"

"Stop it, Pauline!"

Pauline bit her lips. Finally, color returned to her face and she sat up slowly. "What are we going to do?"

"The men have ridden back to the campsite—"

Suzannah stopped, putting a finger to her lips. "I could swear I heard a soft voice in the bushes."

Seconds later, Jamie toddled out. "Ma-ma!" he called happily. "Ma-ma!" His blue homespun shirt and jumper were dirty, but his eyes sparkled.

"Jamie!" Pauline grabbed the little boy and hugged him to her. "Jamie, you're safe!"

"How did you get here, Jamie?" Suzannah wanted to know.

"Da!" he said, and pointed to the bushes.

For an instant, she caught a glimpse of a slight Indian girl in a fringed buckskin dress. The girl's dark eyes met Suzannah's, and she smiled shyly. Then suddenly, without even rustling the bushes, she disappeared.

"Thank you!" Suzannah called after her. "Thank you for bringing Jamie to us!"

The only answer was the whisper of the breeze in the treetops.

Suzannah turned to Pauline who sat on the ground holding Jamie, tears streaming down her face. "It must be the girl Daniel saved," Suzannah said. "She must have found him, then hurried to catch up with us."

But Pauline was still hugging Jamie and crying.

Hoping the search party could still hear her, Suzannah shouted as loudly as she could. "Jamie's been found! Jamie's here!"

She heard Daniel's faint reply. "I'll tell the others!"

She let out a great sigh of relief and turned back to her sister.

"How can I ever forgive myself for not watching you more closely, little pumpkin?" Pauline was murmuring to Jamie. "And with your father gone, how will I ever manage another baby?"

"Another baby?" Suzannah was stunned.

Pauline lifted her blue eyes in dismay. "I didn't mean to tell—I'd never have told if . . . if this hadn't happened.

Promise you won't say anything to Aunt Ruthie or Aunt Pearl or Daniel or *anyone*."

"I promise," Suzannah said, too overcome with the news to speak. People didn't *talk* about having babies. Babies just . . . well, they just suddenly appeared.

"That's why I've been so tired lately," Pauline explained.

An awful feeling swept over Suzannah. Aunt Ruthie and Uncle Franklin were always helpful, but ever since Father and Mother had died in that accident, Pauline (and Charles, of course) had been expected to take care of their family. Now that Charles was gone, who was supposed to take care of Pauline? And what if something happened to Pauline?

As Pauline rose to her feet, Suzannah remembered passing a covered wagon train that had stopped to bury a woman who had died in childbirth. *No!* She refused to think like that. Pauline was young, and she'd probably pull through.

Suddenly, finding gold and settling down were more important than ever. With her sister having a baby and Charles away, Suzannah realized there was only one solution. *She* would have to take charge.

# CHAPTER
# TWO

W agons, ho-o!" Captain Monroe shouted to start the wagon train again. "Wagons, ho-o!"

Suzannah glanced back at the wagon, relieved to see Jamie peeping out from the canvas opening.

Spying the oxen, he waved his arms. "Doggies!"

"Look at him," Suzannah told Daniel. "He doesn't even know the worry and trouble he caused us, wandering off like that."

Daniel nodded, more concerned with the oxen at the moment.

"Doggies!" Jamie yelled again.

It must have been the hundredth time they had corrected him, but this time Suzannah was so glad to see him back that she laughed. "Oxen," she said. "*Oxen*. Lad and Lass are doggies."

Daniel cracked the whip in the air over the oxen's backs. C-r-a-c-k! The sound split the air like a gunshot. "Giddap, boys!" Daniel yelled.

The oxen plodded forward, their heads lowered.

"Ox-*en*," Jamie announced. "Ox-*en*."

Pauline hugged him. "Why, Jamie Herrington. You know a new word!"

"Ox-*en*," he announced again. "Ox-*en!* Ox-*en!*"

Daniel laughed along with Suzannah. "Now we'll probably never hear the end of it."

"Ox-*en!*" Jamie repeated proudly.

Best of all, as far as Suzannah was concerned, Pauline no longer seemed dazed. It was a sweet sight to see her and Jamie together, but a reminder, too, that there would be another baby before long.

Daniel kept an eye on the trail and the oxen. "Tell me again what the Indian girl looked like," he asked Suzannah.

"She had black braids and a deerskin dress with fringe on it," she said slowly, trying to remember the details. "It was such a quick look, though, that I'm not sure of anything except that she smiled at me."

"I bet it was the same girl," he said. "Trying to repay the favor the best she could."

"Maybe so—" It was a wonderful thought. Then suddenly Suzannah could not resist teasing. "Or maybe she's in love with you, Daniel, because you saved her life. Maybe it's an old Indian custom, and she'll follow you all the way to California!"

Grinning, Daniel reached out to tug her pigtail, "You're crazy, Suzannah Elizabeth Colton!"

She dodged him just in time.

At midday, when the wagons stopped for their nooning, the hunting party brought in wild rabbits.

"Thank goodness!" Suzannah said. "My teeth are just about worn down on jerked buffalo."

They were unhitching the oxen when Mordechai, their guide, rode in on No-Name, his brown-spotted pony. The mountain man's deerskin breeches and shirt were grimy, thick with the dust of many a trail. Suzannah wondered if he ever washed his clothes, since he had no wife to help him, or if he just threw them away when they were stiff enough to stand by themselves!

"Circle them wagons tighter!" yelled the grizzled mountain man, his wispy white beard blowing back as he rode around in the circle. "Ye know this here's Bannock Indian country! Ain't ye learned nothin' yit?"

"Old Mordechai would rather yell at us than eat when he's hungry," muttered one of the Murphy boys. "Come on, let's push these wagons closer before he gits too riled up."

While the men tightened the wagon circle, the women and girls got out food and cooking utensils, and the younger boys hunted up wood for the cookfires.

When he was sure that no outsider could break through their defenses, Mordechai rode up to the Colton family cookfire. "Keep them rabbit skins," he said to the women. "They'll come in handy later. We'll do like the Injuns and sew moccasins fer our oxen."

"Moccasins for oxen?" Suzannah couldn't believe her ears.

"Fer crossin' the desert ahead," Mordechai explained. "If we take keer of them oxen, they might git us across that mean stretch of land."

Suzannah turned to Pauline. "Guess we'll be making fur slippers for cattle next!"

Pauline only smiled. "If you'll find greens for dinner, I'll make the rice and get the dishes from the grub box so I can keep an eye on Jamie."

Aunt Ruthie looked up from peeling carrots. "Just don't wander too far, Suzannah."

She grinned. "And miss dinner?"

Her aunt's blue eyes sparkled and she laughed, looking just like Uncle Franklin's pet name for her, "Ruthie Sunshine." "Guess I shouldn't worry. You've yet to miss dinner since the day you were born!"

"And I don't aim to begin today, either!" Suzannah called back.

Leaving the circled wagons, she headed for a spot along the trail where she was sure she had seen some dandelion greens just before they made camp. Humming, she started through the small meadow Ned Taylor was using to pasture the livestock.

"Jamie all right?" Ned asked as he staked a horse to keep him from running off.

"He's fine, thank you," she replied. She realized Ned was staring at her, and it made her feel strange. 'Have you seen any dandelions or other greens around here?"

"Can't say I have. Most of the time, I got all I can do to keep from losin' the livestock."

"I guess you've got your hands full," she replied, spotting some greens beside the trail.

No sooner had she stooped over to pick some than she heard Bridgette Murphy, who was fourteen, and the prettiest girl in the wagon train.

"Well, *hello*, Ned Taylor," she said, her voice sounding strangely sweet and musical.

"'Lo, Bridgette."

"Are you getting lonesome back here all by yourself?"

Suzannah rolled her eyes skyward. Ned wasn't alone, she thought. He had some thirty head of cattle to keep him company.

Ned turned red and and tied another horse to a stake.

Bridgette sauntered over a little closer. "I do like red-headed men, especially when their hair is curly."

*Men*? Ned was fifteen, probably not even full grown.

Suzannah glanced over at them. Ned's face was about the color of his flaming hair, and he took a swipe at his hair. She wondered if he'd say he liked beautiful black-haired girls with violet eyes—like Bridgette—but he didn't.

"Well, Suzannah," the girl said in her new musical voice, "are you picking *all* the greens?"

"I left some," Suzannah replied shortly. "That why *you're* here?"

Bridgette blinked her long dark lashes at Ned. "Why else would I come back here?"

Suzannah shrugged. "Didn't notice you looking for greens, so I wouldn't know."

Bridgette's violet eyes hardened like stones, and her voice turned hard. "Little girls shouldn't wander so far from home."

"I didn't know you cared," Suzannah retorted. Then, spotting a big patch of greens, she hurried away.

Later, when she looked behind her, she saw Ned Taylor helping Bridgette search for salad greens. Hmmph! If he could be fooled by a silly, vain girl like that, well, he wasn't the boy she thought he was.

As Suzannah finished her chore, she felt as if someone were watching her from the woods. She darted a glance at Bridgette and Ned, but they were too busy to notice. In the nearby forest, the trees and bushes stood absolutely still in the heat of the midday sun. No hint of a breeze touched the leaves. Suddenly a tree branch moved, its leaves fluttering slightly. *Indians*, she thought. *Indians!*

She turned and started back toward the campsite, trying not to appear rushed. She put one foot in front of the other. One step at a time. It seemed forever before she neared the wagon circle. Finally she stepped between the wagons and rushed into the middle of the circle.

"Mordechai!" she called. "Mordechai!"

She was glad to see the old guide on No-Name talking to the hunting party, all mounted on their horses. Among them was Uncle Karl, Aunt Pearl's new husband, a rangy, dark-haired man who wasn't any too friendly.

Suzannah raced over to them. "Someone in the forest was watching me pick greens along the trail."

"Ye sure?" Mordechai asked, squinting at her through his beady eyes.

"Well . . . not positive. But a branch moved and leaves fluttered . . . and there *wasn't any breeze*."

Mordechai squared his shoulders under his old buckskin shirt. "Don't worry, we'll see to it."

Uncle Karl glowered at her from beneath his dark brows. "Hope you ain't sendin' us on a wild goose chase, girl!"

"I wouldn't do it on purpose. But there was *something* in those woods," she replied, trying to hold her temper.

"Suzannah ain't flighty," Mordechai said to the men. "If she says there's somethin', we'd best take a look."

Motioning to the riders, he turned back to the emigrants gathered around. "Stay put 'n keep yer eyes peeled fer trouble. These fellers 'n me are goin' back down the trail a piece."

The other men grabbed their rifles from their wagons and looked out beyond the wagon circle. Uncle Karl gave Suzannah another dark look before he and the rest of the hunting party rode off with Mordechai, their rifles handy, Lad and Lass nipping at their heels.

Garth, who was as tall and bony as Uncle Karl, gave her a dark look, too, then stationed himself between two wagons, his rifle cocked and ready.

"You don't have to be mad at me," she told him.

"Ain't mad."

"Glad to hear it. Maybe you just got a habit of looking grouchy then."

"Could be. I'm tryin' to unlearn it."

When he actually smiled at her, her mouth dropped open in surprise. Didn't that beat all! Come to think of it, he didn't seem quite as angry as when she'd first met him. In fact, ever since he'd almost shot that Indian girl, he'd shown signs of softening. Now he sometimes held Aunt Pearl's hand when they said grace before meals, and he'd even gone to the worship service yesterday.

At the cookfire, Suzannah tried to stay busy helping her aunts and Pauline make dinner, but they were all watching for Mordechai and the hunting party. Finally, when the rabbit stew was almost ready, Mordechai and the others rode back into the wagon circle.

"Didn't find nobody," he said. "Could've been an animal Suzanny heerd. But thet don't mean we shouldn't keep our eyes and ears open wide."

Uncle Karl dismounted and tied his horse to the wagon wheel, muttering under his breath. "Struck me as a wild goose chase."

That afternoon, as their covered wagons rolled southward along the Raft River, Suzannah again felt someone's eyes on her from the woods across the stream.

"Don't you feel someone watching us?" she asked Daniel. She was almost afraid to hear his answer. What if he thought her imagination was running away with her, as Mother used to say?

He darted a glance across the stream. "Mordechai says the Indians are always watching. Says they know when intruders are about. I think he's worried about the Bannocks."

Day by day the trail grew rougher as they climbed higher and higher. It took off along Cassia Creek and headed for a rock formation Mordechai called the "City of Rocks." When they arrived there, Suzannah stared at miles of gray granite columns rising from the floor of the valley below. The outcroppings looked like great mansions in the midst of a large, green park. At the southern edge of the silent city, twin spires named Cathedral Rocks pierced the blue sky. It was such an awesome place that the others seemed to forget all about the Indians, but Suzannah still couldn't shake the feeling that someone was watching them.

During their nooning in the City of Rocks, she sat under a gnarled juniper tree with Pauline, Aunt Ruthie, and Aunt Pearl. The shade was a blessed relief from the August heat, even if they did have to sew rabbit skin moccasins for the oxen's feet.

"Wouldn't our friends in Alexandria laugh their heads off if they could see us now?" Suzannah said.

"They'd be shocked is more like it," Pauline answered. But she was smiling. In fact, sitting there stitching at a moccasin, she had never looked prettier. So peaceful and content. Not like when Charles was around to keep her flustered and upset.

"I can imagine them discussing our sewing 'bees' at the Alexandria teas," Pauline added.

"We should make some moccasins for Lad and Lass, too," Suzannah joked.

Pauline laughed, seeming more like her old self than she had in a long time.

Suzannah set to work on a new moccasin. First, she cut a piece of fur and made small holes around the edges. Next, she laced a narrow strip of leather through the holes to make a drawstring. They'd put the furry side around the ox's hoof, pull the lace up tight, and tie it.

As she threaded a strip of leather through a lacing hole, she was thinking what Mordechai had said about the moccasins. "Make 'em good and strong. We're countin' on them moccasins to help the critters git us through thet turrible desert."

Suzannah said, "I don't like to think about that desert ahead."

"Then don't," her sister answered. "Set your mind on other things. The apostle Paul said, 'Whatsoever things are true, whatsoever things are honest, whatsoever things are just, whatsoever things are pure, whatsoever things are lovely, whatsoever things are of good report . . . if there be any virtue, and if there be any praise, think on these things.'"

Suzannah guessed that was how her sister coped with being married to Charles Herrington—keeping her mind on other things.

Beyond the City of Rocks, the trail dipped into a broad valley, then climbed another high divide before it dropped sharply down to Goose Creek.

"We're almost to the end of Bannock Injun country," Mordechai said. "I figger they might still give us trouble, though. They ain't known fer bein' peaceable. Keep them collie dogs close to yer wagon."

At midday, as Suzannah set out to find salad greens,

she sent Lad and Lass back. "Go home . . . go to the wagons!" But she wished she had let them come with her when she left the safety of the wagon circle and once again had the sense of being watched. When she passed Ned Taylor in the makeshift corral, she asked him if he felt the same thing.

"Can't say I do," he replied. "You scared?"

"Not a bit!" she retorted a little too loudly. "Well, I'm going down to Goose Creek for greens."

"Watch out for rattlesnakes by the water."

"I'm not scared of them, either," she sniffed. "I'm just mighty careful of them." She hurried past him and the livestock, heading for the narrow creek.

When she arrived, only the chirping of birds in the trees broke the midday stillness. She made her way carefully through the thicket of bushes and saplings to the grasses by the creek. No sooner had she begun tearing off the tender greens than she heard a soft rustle in the grass. Lifting her head cautiously, she almost dropped the greens from her hands.

An Indian girl stood before her, her soft dark eyes watching her. She was graceful as a doe, and beautiful— with her glossy black braids, her beaded deerskin dress and moccasins.

"Aren't you . . . the girl Daniel saved, the one who brought Jamie back to us?" Suzannah whispered.

The girl lifted a hand to show she didn't understand. Then she murmured a few words in her language and presented Suzannah with a basket of choice greens.

Suzannah pointed to herself. "For me?"

The girl nodded, then brought her hands together, opening them wider and wider.

"For my family, too," Suzannah guessed. "For Daniel, Pauline, and Jamie—" She made a motion with her hands, stretching to show a person Daniel's height,

then lowering her hand to Pauline's height, then lower still for Jamie.

The girl flashed a brilliant white smile.

"So *you're* the one who's been watching us," Suzannah said, knowing the girl didn't understand a word she was saying. "You've seen our family together . . . how much Pauline loves Jamie—"

Suddenly the girl's eyes darted past Suzannah and her smile faded. She took a few steps backward, whirled, and disappeared into the thicket of bushes.

"Thank you for all you've done!" Suzannah called after her.

Daniel and Ned appeared in the little clearing and rushed to her side. "The Indian girl!"

"It *was.* . . . until you two scared her off!"

"I wanted to try to talk to her," Daniel said, and hurried into the thicket along Goose Creek.

Suzannah decided not to follow. After all, Daniel was the one who had saved her life.

"Did *you* see her?" she asked Ned.

"Just barely."

"I guess she'd already done what she set out to do. She gave me this beautiful basket of greens," Suzannah explained. "She must have seen me looking for them before. I wish we could really be friends."

"Expect she won't forget you and Daniel, either," Ned said. "I know *I* won't."

Suzannah gave him a curious look. "Well, I know why you won't forget Daniel. After all, he saved your life—" She was recalling the river crossing when Daniel had rescued Ned from drowning. "But *I* haven't done anything—"

"Oh, yes you have!" Ned spoke up, then blushed beet red. "That is, you and your whole family. What I mean is . . . you're fine folks."

For some reason, Suzannah just had to ask. "What about Bridgette Murphy?"

Ned ducked his head and ran his hand through his red curls, making them spring up wilder than ever. "Aw, you don't need to worry about Bridgette Murphy."

"Thank you, Ned," Suzannah said softly, not feeling like joking at all. "Guess . . . guess I'd better get back now."

*Fine folks.* Suzannah thought over what Ned had said as she walked slowly back to the circled wagons with the basket of greens on her arm. Ned liked her family. He'd said so more than once. Did the Indian girl feel that way, too?

Shortly afterward, Daniel caught up with her, all out

of breath. "I couldn't find her, but I saw her long enough in the clearing to know she was the one, all right."

"I think she's been watching the wagon train all along, to be sure we were safe."

Daniel nodded. "Giving us safe conduct through Bannock country."

"And she gave me this basket and the greens."

"She must have wanted us to have something to remember her by."

"I'll never forget her. Never." They walked on toward the wagon circle in silence until Suzannah spoke up again. "I suppose she's not a Christian, is she?"

Daniel thought for a minute. "I suppose not. But it's a funny thing. Reverend Benjamin says pagans can be good people, too. And some people who claim to be church-going Christians don't truly know Christ at all . . . and can be just awful."

"Well, that Indian girl is a kind person, for sure. But you were good to her. You saved her life."

Daniel nodded thoughtfully, not with pride. "She might have thought she was returning a favor, but her watching over us the way she did makes me think of God guiding His people through the wilderness. And of His promise never to leave us or forsake us."

They fell silent again, and the beauty of the sky, trees, and mountains spoke to them about God and how well He had taken care of them so far.

*I thank Thee, Lord, for keeping us safe,* Suzannah prayed. *Please help us, especially Pauline and her baby, as we cross the desert and the Sierra Nevada Mountains. If it's true, like Mordechai says, that the worst of the journey is still ahead, we're going to need Thee even more.*

# CHAPTER
# THREE

They spent the next Sabbath, August thirteenth, resting near Goose Creek. Uncle Franklin led the worship service and spoke on trusting God, no matter what happened. Aunt Pearl led the singing of the hymns, including Suzannah's favorite, "Amazing Grace."

That evening when Mordechai inspected the oxen, he rubbed his scrawny beard as he observed Rose, Iris, Daisy, Marigold, Sweet Pea, and Dandelion. "They're thinner, but considerin' all, in tolerable condition."

"They're well-trained, too," Suzannah assured him. And since there was no one else around, she added, "They even hold still for me to yoke them. I believe I could drive them myself."

Mordechai lifted a wiry eyebrow. "Can ye crack the whip without tearin' their backs to ribbons?"

"I think so," she said. "I've been watching Daniel. And I've been practicing in the meadows."

The old guide ventured a smile. "I expect ye can try it. If ye can bullwhack that wagon, we could make good use of Dan'l as a lookout rider. He tells me he'd like to try ridin' fer a while."

Uncle Franklin must have overheard them as he rode up, for he reminded Mordechai: "This is the lead wagon tomorrow. The rest of our family's wagons rotate to the rear of the train."

Mordechai gave a nod. "Yep. I know. But unless yer objectin', I'd like to try Suzanny as a bullwhacker. The more folks as kin take a turn, the easier it'll be if we run into real trouble. I heerd yer fine prayin' this morning, and I expect ye could pray her through the day."

Uncle Franklin had to smile a little. "Well, just for a few days then. I wouldn't want her to take that kind of responsibility for long."

Suzannah kept still, though she really wanted to tell Uncle Franklin that she knew all about responsibility. Since Charles had ridden off with those gold miners, she had taken on the responsibility of his family!

"I'll be ridin' in front fer a ways," Mordechai said. "Then Captain Monroe will lead. We'll give 'er a try."

Uncle Franklin gave her a long appraising look. "Fact is, I wouldn't be surprised if she does just fine."

"Dead right," Mordechai agreed, "even if she *is* just workin' her way up to bein' a woman."

Suzannah felt a hot flush rise to her cheeks.

Uncle Franklin laughed, then suggested, "Let's keep your new job a secret from Pauline and your aunts until morning so they don't lose any sleep."

"Best not to tell them until I'm actually up there bullwhacking," she agreed. "If I know them, they'll say it's too dangerous and unladylike."

Uncle Franklin clapped her on the shoulder. "Your father would be mighty proud of you, Suzannah."

"But I'm not so sure about Mother."

"Oh, I believe she would approve, too," he assured her. "If I remember correctly, your mother had a little tomboy in her, too!"

The next morning, the news that Suzannah would be bullwhacking got out at breakfast.

"You can't be serious!" Pauline protested, a spoonful of porridge halfway to Jamie's mouth. "Girls just don't do things like that!"

Suzannah's heart sank. She could see that Aunt Ruthie was about to agree, so she gulped down the rest of her flapjacks and hurried out to do her chores before anything more could be said. But before she was out of earshot, her other aunt surprised her.

"I'm sure Suzannah can bullwhack a team as well as a boy," said Aunt Pearl. "And Daniel is needed as a lookout rider, I hear."

*Bless Aunt Pearl's heart!* Suzannah thought gratefully. With this encouragement, she rushed to the wagon and set to work with the oxen, hoping she wouldn't disappoint anyone. And when Captain Monroe yelled, "Catch up! Catch up!" she already had the oxen yoked.

Since the lead driver didn't dare keep the others waiting, she worked as fast as she could. In no time at all, the oxen and wagon were in place at the head of the wagon train.

"Are you sure you want to try this?" called Pauline, peering out the canvas flap. She had a worried look on her face. "What if Marigold sits down again?"

Suzannah thought of that embarrassing day, several

months ago, when Marigold had staged a sit-down strike
on the trail outside of Independence, Missouri. It had
taken all the strength and cleverness Daniel could muster
to get him up again.

Suzannah shook off the embarrassing memory. "Stop
it, Pauline! Why can't you be like Aunt Pearl? She has faith
in me."

"She's a country woman. She's used to such work."

"Then maybe I take after her!" said Suzannah, then
was sorry she had sounded so irritable. After all, Pauline
was feeling poorly this morning, as she usually did now
because of the baby. "Besides . . . well, I've prayed about
it. And I hope you'll pray for me, too."

With these words, Suzannah felt a surge of
confidence. Taking her stand next to the wheel team, Iris
and Marigold, she lifted the long black bullwhip.

Three lookout riders mounted their horses and cantered off into the dry, dusty land ahead, while Daniel rode
with Captain Monroe alongside the wagons.

"You ready?" Daniel asked Suzannah.

"I'm ready," she replied, relieved that Pauline was no
longer putting up an argument.

Before long, Captain Monroe rode out in front.
"Wagons, ho-o!"

Now was the moment! Suzannah sent up another
prayer, muttering under her breath, "Marigold, don't fail
me now!"

"Giddup, boys! Giddup!" she yelled. She flung out
the bullwhip, which curled menacingly in the air over the
oxen, leaping out at least a foot above their backs. Its crack
sounded just right, like a gunshot.

As the weight of the oxen's massive shoulders fell
against the yokes, the wagon groaned and lurched forward.
Lad and Lass barked wildly, but despite the barking dogs,
the oxen plodded on.

"You did it, Sue!" Pauline exclaimed from inside the wagon. "You did it!'"

"You could have done it, too, if you had to," said Suzannah, walking beside the steadily moving oxen. "Especially if you had prayed as hard as I have."

Following Captain Monroe on his horse, Suzannah glanced back to see the wagons falling into line behind them.

Just then Mordechai rode by with Daniel. "Good job!" their guide called to her. "I knew ye could do it."

Daniel grinned. "She's a Colton, isn't she?"

"I've been watching *you*," she admitted to her cousin, and he looked more pleased than ever.

Suzannah felt herself grinning, too. Ladylike or not, it sure was a powerful feeling to set an entire wagon train in motion! Still, without the inner peace the Lord had given her, she'd never have tried it.

"I'll be scoutin' ahead now," Mordechai said. "Next tribe of Injuns we come to will be the Shoshones, best known as 'Diggers'."

Suzannah was curious. "Diggers?"

"They dig in the ground fer their vittles . . . roots 'n grubs 'n sech."

"They eat *grubs?*"

He laughed at the wry face she made. "Ain't the worst of it. They'll eat anythin' they kin git their hands on—even grasshoppers and rats!"

"Aaugh!"

"They ain't warlike," he went on, "but they don't understand 'bout personal property. Keep a watch on the horses and oxen, and don't hang out yer clothes on the bushes to dry or they'll steal 'em right off."

"Guess I won't be hanging out any clothes to dry as long as I'm bullwhacking," she told him. "But I'll warn Pauline, Aunt Ruthie, and Aunt Pearl."

Mordechai nodded and rode ahead on No-Name. "Don't let up on them oxen," he called back.

As they moved on, Suzannah squinted into the bright sunlight. Although grass grew along the streams off Goose Creek, the uplands were more desertlike, with dry grass, sagebrush, and prickly pear cactus dotting the landscape. Now, on top of all that, there were the Digger Indians.

"Giddup, boys!" she called out to the oxen to keep them moving at a steady pace. "Giddup for California! It's bound to be an improvement over this country!"

As the morning hours passed, Suzannah had to slow down only once when she came to a rained-out gully, but the men quickly shoveled dirt to build it up, and the wagons rolled over it with ease. By their midday stop, however, the desert heat had sapped her strength.

"You want Daniel to take the team again?" Captain Monroe asked.

"Not yet," she decided, fanning her hot face with her sunbonnet. "If the Diggers are as bad as Mordechai says, Daniel will be more useful as a lookout."

"You're right about that," the captain answered.

Instead of helping the women cook the midday meal, Suzannah busied herself with the oxen, feeding and watering them and tending to their cuts. She was cleaning out Sweet Pea's hooves when Pauline arrived, holding her blue calico dress up carefully as she brought Suzannah a tin cup of buttermilk.

Her older sister grimaced. "I don't know how you can handle those dirty things!"

"I'm getting used to it. At least it's not as much work as Ned has, with a whole pasture full of loose livestock to keep up with."

"I suppose not," Pauline replied, waiting for Suzannah to drink the buttermilk. "But nowadays, he gets a lot of encouragement from Bridgette Murphy."

Suzannah stopped drinking, mid-gulp. "What do you mean?"

Pauline shrugged. "Only that Bridgette brings him food and water each day when we stop to rest. Everyone in the wagon train has noticed it."

The buttermilk soured in her mouth, but Suzannah drained the cup dry. Here she was bullwhacking the wagon train's lead team of oxen like a grown man, while Bridgette was batting her long black lashes at Ned Taylor like a grown woman!

"Why tell *me?*" Suzannah asked, thrusting the empty cup back at her sister.

"Just thought you might be interested."

"Well, I'm not!" Suzannah snapped. She finished cleaning Sweet Pea's hoof, then changed the subject. "Before long, we'll have to put the rabbit fur moccasins on the oxen's hooves. This dryness is hard on them."

"It's hard on our skin, too, Suzannah," Pauline said. "You'd better keep your sunbonnet up. You'll notice that Bridgette Murphy does."

Suzannah winced. After a moment, she said, "Thanks for the buttermilk. You feeling all right?"

Pauline nodded. "Better than this morning."

But Suzannah didn't put up her sunbonnet until mid-afternoon when the desert sun slanted its burning rays from the west. It was hard work, keeping the lead oxen going at a good pace. Usually they kept up with the wagon in front of them, but without another wagon to set the pace, they tended to lag.

By early evening, she'd had enough of bullwhacking for one day and was glad when Daniel rode back with three rabbits for supper.

"I'll tend to the oxen if you'll skin these rabbits," he said.

"Me . . . skin rabbits?"

He gave a short laugh. "Then ask Aunt Pearl to do it. She's used to it. After bullwhacking all day, maybe they'll give you a sitting-down job, like peeling potatoes."

Suzannah grabbed the rabbits by their hind legs, too tired to discuss skinning them or anything else.

Aunt Pearl took one look at her and issued a stern order. "Suzannah Colton, go rest in the wagon with Jamie, while Ruthie and I cook supper."

Suzannah was only too happy to obey, and she climbed into the wagon and promptly fell asleep on the quilts beside her little nephew. She would probably have slept right through supper, too, if Jamie hadn't poked her awake, yelling in her ear: "Get up, 'Zanna! Get up!"

The next morning Suzannah again agreed to be the bullwhacker for their wagon, even though rotating to the back meant they would travel in the other wagons' dust. Ned was just behind her with what was left of the loose livestock—horses, milk cows, a few beef cattle, and eight spare oxen who'd become too weak to pull the wagons.

Now and then, when the wagon train halted, she gave him a sidelong look, remembering what Bridgette Murphy had said in her musical voice: "I *do* like red-headed men!"

Nothing Suzannah could think to say to him seemed very interesting after that. So she said the first thing that came to mind: "You don't have nearly so much livestock to watch now, do you?"

"Makes it all the more important to watch 'em," he replied. "We can't afford to lose any more."

Despite the dust, she couldn't help admiring the way his red hair curled over his ears. All of a sudden she blushed, realizing he was looking at her curiously.

"Mordechai says Diggers will steal clothes right off

the creek bushes while they're hanging up to dry!" she blurted.

"Worse than that," Ned said mysteriously.

"What's worse?"

"It's best I don't tell."

Just then Bridgette Murphy arrived with a cup of water for Ned. "Don't tell her what?" she teased.

Ned's eyes wandered over both of them, considering. "Guess I'm too thirsty to talk."

Bridgette smiled prettily. "You can't have any water, Ned Taylor, unless you promise to tell."

He reached for the cup. "You won't want to hear it."

Bridgette backed away, keeping the cup just out of his reach. "You have to promise, Ned Taylor, or I will never ever bring you water again."

He drew a deep breath. "I promise. But I warn you. You won't like it one bit."

Bridgette gave him the water and stood watching him drink, her pretty head tilted, her hands on the hips of her yellow gingham dress.

Suzannah stepped back, feeling like one person too many . . . especially in her faded red calico. Still, she'd been there first.

Finally Ned downed the last swig of water, and swiped at his mouth with the back of his hand.

"Well?" Bridgette asked.

Ned shook his head.

"But you promised!"

"Shouldn't have."

Bridgette turned to Suzannah. "What were you two talkin' about?"

"About the Digger Indians stealing clothes off the creek bushes when they're hung out to dry."

Bridgette's violet eyes narrowed as she regarded Ned. "And what else?"

"You asked for it," Ned cautioned. "The fact is, Mordechai says those Indians will dig up emigrants' graves for the clothes *right off their corpses!*"

Suzannah swallowed hard.

Beside her, Bridgette gasped. "Oh, Ned . . . I do believe . . . I'm going to faint."

She took two steps toward Ned, then swayed in his direction. He grabbed her before she hit the ground.

"Why, Bridgette Murphy," Suzannah scolded, "you got that idea from Pauline fainting when Jamie was lost! Only Pauline didn't do it on *purpose!*"

The girl's violet eyes blinked open for an instant, then she remembered to close them.

Disgusted, Suzannah didn't even look at Ned as she turned and headed for her wagon. Once there, she glanced back over her shoulder and saw him fanning Bridgette's face with his hat. And, behind them, a band of half-naked Indians creeping up on the loose livestock.

"Indians!" Suzannah shouted. "Indians! Indians in the meadow!"

Pauline took up the cry. "Help, someone! Indians!"

Soon the alarm could be heard up and down the line of wagons. "Indians! Indians!"

Bridgette jumped up as quickly as she had fainted and ran for the safety of her family's wagon.

In moments, the dogs were all barking, and the outriders rode back, shooting their rifles into the air. In the midst of the racket, Ned mounted his horse and corraled the livestock, while the other men chased the Indians to a distant gully.

Before long, the men returned, riding hard. "We've scared them off for now," Captain Monroe said. "I don't think they'll bother us again for a while, but we'll have to stay alert until we reach the mountains." Looking over at

Ned, he nodded in approval. "Good thing you saw them, young fellow."

Red-faced, Ned shook his head. "It was Suzannah Colton who sounded the alarm."

Captain Monroe turned an appreciative gaze on her. "Then our thanks to you, Miss Colton. The Diggers aren't apt to kill us, but they'll happily steal our livestock and food, which makes them just as dangerous in the end."

She nodded, but kept her mouth shut. At the moment, she didn't know who was more dangerous— Bridgette Murphy or the Digger Indians!

"It's just as easy to bullwhack as it is to walk beside the wagons," Suzannah decided after the first two days.

"Reckon I'll try it a spell, then," Aunt Pearl said. "That'll free Garth for hunting. We're low on meat."

"Guess I could try it, too," Aunt Ruthie said.

Uncle Franklin cast a worried eye at her. "Not for long, though. But if you can manage a little while, Ruthie, it would allow me to ride in back and help Ned Taylor guard the livestock."

Despite their worry over the Diggers, the next three days were easy going. But when they hit the Humboldt River, the hot desert sun baked the life out of all of them— animals and humans alike.

"Ye might as well git used to it," Mordechai said. "There's over three hunderd more miles jest like it. It'll take us the better part of three weeks."

"The 'Humbug' don't even look like a river," grumbled Uncle Karl, making the grim news worse, "not after you've seen the Mississippi or even the Missouri. It don't run like a river, and there ain't one fish in it nor another livin' thing."

Suzannah had to agree. But, by now, the travelers in the wagon train didn't look so good either. All of them were tired and dusty, beaten down by the long miles and hot sun. Still, they kept on, toiling through the gray sagebrush and cactus, always on the lookout for the Diggers.

To make matters worse, Pauline was feeling poorly most of the time now. She seldom sat on the driver's seat to sketch the mountains on either side of them as they rumbled across the forbidding country.

"They're beautiful mountains," she said, "but I'm just not in the mood to draw."

Suzannah was worried about her sister. "Pauline, that doesn't sound like you at all."

Pauline shook her head. "I guess I don't feel much like myself, either."

*Lord, help us get through this,* Suzannah prayed again and again.

The days seemed endless as she trudged alongside the wagon. At mealtime, there was usually jack-rabbit stew— the toughest, most awful-tasting meat she'd ever eaten. And when the Humboldt River turned from milky-white to yellowish-green, they had to bring out lemon acid from the medicine chests and add a few drops to the river water to make it drinkable.

Even at that, Uncle Karl was doubtful "Most likely we're poisonin' ourselves and the livestock with this water."

*And Pauline and her baby,* Suzannah thought.

When they came to the evil-smelling Humboldt Sink, the murky river disappeared into soggy marshes. And that night, when it was pitch dark, the Diggers stole two horses and Aunt Ruthie's milk cow.

"Afraid that means no more milk for Jamie," Uncle Franklin said.

*Or for Pauline and the baby,* Suzannah thought.

With so many troubles, she scarcely even noticed or cared anymore whether Bridgette Murphy was carrying water to Ned Taylor.

"Forty-Mile Desert dead ahead!" called Mordechai one day. "We'll stop here to cut all the grass we kin carry fer the livestock. And be sure to store up plenty of water fer them and fer yerselves. The Humboldt River ain't much, but it's all the water ye'll be seein' fer some time."

"And now's the time to get out the rabbit-fur moccasins for the oxen's feet," added Captain Monroe.

Suzannah darted a worried glance at Pauline, who looked paler than ever, in spite of the sun bearing down on them day after day. *What if she dies?* Suzannah asked herself. If Pauline didn't live, Suzannah would have to take care of Jamie . . . and maybe the new baby, too!

Shaking off the frightening thought, Suzannah got busy. "If you can find the oxen's moccasins in the wagon," she told her sister, "I'll see about getting grass and water."

Pauline's eyes filled with tears. "I know I'm not doing my share, and I feel bad about it."

"Just take care of Jamie and . . . and the baby!" Suzannah replied, dropping her voice to a whisper almost too late. She looked around, grateful no one had overheard.

"I just hope the baby doesn't come when we're going through the mountains," Pauline said. "I can feel it moving now."

"Have you told anyone else about it?"

Pauline shook her head. "They'd just be madder than ever at Charles for leaving—"

Suzannah bit her tongue to keep from saying something hateful. She herself had been furious with Charles for riding ahead to the gold fields and leaving his family behind. But now she was too tired to think of him much. For all she knew, they might never even see him again. Instead, she had to keep her mind on stocking up for the long trek through the desert, then tying the rabbit fur moccasins on the oxen—

"We'll start into the desert at first light," Mordechai told them as he rode by the wagons that afternoon. "Won't be no time fer cookin' breakfast, so make extra biscuits tonight. And we'd best git to bed early, so won't be no singin' 'round the campfire."

"We haven't had any singing since the Rocky Mountains," Suzannah grumbled, tying the last of the moccasins on Marigold's hooves.

Mordechai must have overheard her complaint, for he said, "I already give in to yer restin' on the Sabbath. I don't mean to take no other chances."

Shading her eyes against the burning glare of hot sun on desert sand, Suzannah urged the oxen forward. The land, baked hard and dry, leveled out all around and was covered with white alkaline. By mid-morning, each step seared her feet and each hour seemed to stretch out into forever.

At the suggestion of Captain Monroe, the emigrants put pebbles under their tongues to help keep their mouths wet, but it didn't help much. The dogs, yipping in pain from the hot sand, had to ride in Aunt Pearl's wagon. When the sun was directly overhead, Suzannah's eyes swam and dots danced across the dry land.

"Well, at least we've probably lost the Digger Indians," Suzannah said to Daniel as he rode by.

He nodded wearily. "Can't even see lizards or rattlesnakes around here."

That night Captain Monroe had to shoot four dying oxen.

"They're better off, poor things." Suzannah sighed, hoping their animals would fare better.

The next morning Pauline called from the wagon, "Look! There's a lake ahead . . . and trees! Just look at the blue water!"

"It's only a mirage," Uncle Franklin explained to Suzannah.

Suzannah squinted through the dust. Yes, she could see a lake or a wide river, bordered by trees, shimmering in the distance. She blinked and looked again. This time it was gone.

"Lots of people see them," he went on. "I think they're caused by the heat rising from the surface of the land, and a person's own exhaustion."

She decided to let her sister enjoy the mirage a while longer. "Why don't you sketch what you see?"

For the first time in several days, Pauline got out her sketchbook and began to draw. Then suddenly she gave up in tears, and lay down to rest with Jamie.

As the day wore on, some of the emigrants wanted to turn back. "It's too much . . . too much!" they cried. "We should have kept on for Oregon. What good will all of the gold in the world do if we die here in this desert?"

All the next day they traveled in silence across a sandy ridge.

"Rose and Iris are sinking in the sand!" Suzannah called out as she saw the oxen's hooves disappear beneath the top crust.

By the time Uncle Franklin rode back, there was nothing he could do to help. They watched the oxen struggle, bellowing pitifully as they thrashed about, their legs broken.

"Go sit in the wagon with Pauline and Jamie," Uncle Franklin instructed. "Daniel and I will take care of this."

Numb, Suzannah climbed into the wagon, its white top tan from the dust that clung to everything. She lay down carefully, so as not to disturb Pauline and Jamie, who were asleep.

She could feel the wagon shudder as Daniel and Uncle Franklin unhitched the struggling oxen, then heard the shots ring out. Tears filled her eyes for Rose and Iris, but the heat dried the tears before they touched her cheeks. *You can't even grieve properly in this dreadful desert*, she thought angrily.

She didn't get out of the wagon until they were well underway—and she didn't look back. *Lord, get us through this awful place*, she prayed. *Lord, help us!*

The next afternoon she caught sight of cottonwood trees along a river. "Another mirage?" she asked Uncle Franklin.

"I don't think so," he said, shading his eyes with his hand and looking into the distance.

At that moment, Captain Monroe answered their question. "Hold on! Truckee River ahead! We're almost to California!"

*California!* Suzannah felt her spirits lift a little. Maybe they'd make it, after all. She glanced up toward the wagon, but Pauline was nowhere in sight. Her sister was probably napping, as she did most of the time now.

When the oxen caught the scent of water, they began to run.

"Whoa, boys! Whoa!" Suzannah called out, but there was no stopping them until they reached the river.

As soon as they were released from their hitches, the

big animals waded into the water and began to drink deeply. Lad and Lass bounded in behind them, lapping up the cool water with parched tongues.

Mordechai met them at the river. "Well, ye made it this far, I see. Now we'll take a few days' rest."

Suzannah dipped up tin cups of water for Pauline and Jamie, then woke them. "Did you hear that? We've come to the Truckee River," she told her sister. "We're in California!"

Pauline blinked vacantly. And it was all Suzannah could do to get her to drink.

# CHAPTER
# FOUR

It was a steady uphill climb into the Sierra Nevada Mountains. Sagebrush and scrubby pines gave way to patches of forest along the Truckee River, and there was plenty of water and grass again for the oxen.

"Isn't it wonderful to see real trees again?" Suzannah called to Pauline. "And smell that fresh air! We can actually take a deep breath without swallowing sand! Sure beats the desert, doesn't it?"

Pauline only stared into the distance as if she hadn't heard a word.

*Lord, please take care of my sister,* Suzannah prayed again and again. *Maybe You could let Jamie cheer her up . . . and one more thing, please let the baby be all right, too—*

She was relieved when Daniel was no longer needed as a lookout and could help with the river crossings as they

49

crossed and recrossed the Truckee, always climbing higher into the mountains. There was no time to lose now, since Mordechai wanted them to be through the Sierras before heavy snows fell. Snow came early in the mountains, he had reminded the travelers, nd it was already mid September.

"Giddup, boys! Giddup!" they yelled.

But the four remaining oxen—Daisy, Marigold, Sweet Pea, and Dandelion—balked each time they came to the river. They seemed to dislike the cold mountain water as much as Suzannah did. Not only did it chill her legs and keep her skirt and moccasins wet, but she had to struggle against its strong downhill current.

"Giddup!" she and Daniel shouted, tugging and coaxing the oxen.

"There better be plenty of gold left in California to make up for this!" she declared.

"Guess we'll see when we get there," Daniel replied. "What's important now is getting to the top . . . nine thousand feet up."

"I see snow!" she said, pointing to a nearby peak.

Towering high above the timberline, it was a majestic sight to see—the heavy snow icing the peak like a giant birthday cake. But it was a fearsome sight, too.

"We don't want to get snowed in . . . like Mose Schallenberger did," Daniel said.

Suzannah shivered. "Who's he?"

Daniel looked as if he might be wondering whether he should tell, then finally he shrugged and went ahead. "Mose Schallenberger was a boy who traveled with the Stevens Party in '44."

"And they got snowbound . . . in these very mountains?"

Her cousin nodded. "But not right away. They were fine until they got up high. Then, when the snowstorms hit, they decided to send a few people for help. Only no one ever came." He darted Suzannah a quick look to see how she was taking his tale so far.

"Finally," Daniel continued, "the rest of the emigrants packed up their horses and mules and went for help, but they left three of the younger fellows behind with the heavier wagons and most of their valuables."

"Was Mose Schallenberger one of them?"

Daniel nodded. "They built a log cabin and roofed it with hides and pine boughs, even a log chimney faced with stones. But they'd no more than finished it when a worse storm broke. They got three feet of snow the first night."

"Three feet of snow in one night?"

"Yep. Mose and the two others were surprised, but not too worried. The weather wasn't real cold yet, and they thought the snow would melt. But more storms hit."

Suzannah was beginning to get scared. "What time of year was that?"

"November."

"Thank goodness, it's only September!" she exclaimed in relief.

"They started out in May . . . like we did."

Suzannah shivered.

"There was plenty of bedding from the six wagons they were guarding, and they slaughtered two cows for meat. But it kept on snowing, and the stuff was so fluffy they couldn't walk on it."

Suzannah wasn't sure she wanted to hear what happened next, but curiosity kept her from stopping Daniel.

"The two older fellows knew about snowshoes," he continued, "so they took some of the wagon bows and bent them into shape. Then they filled them in with rawhide thongs. I guess they had a time learning to use their new snowshoes, but when they ran out of food, they used them to go out hunting for game. The trouble was, the deer and most of the other animals had already moved down the mountain to find food."

"Then what?"

"It snowed for weeks and weeks, and when they made a fire for warmth, it burned a hole through the snow fifteen feet deep."

"Fifteen feet?" Suzannah's eyes were wide.

"Fifteen feet," Daniel repeated. "When the weather didn't get any better, and they realized that no one was coming back for them, they decided they'd strike out, too, and leave the wagons behind. Well, Mose wasn't any good at snowshoeing. He tried, but all he did was to get muscle cramps trying to stay up, so finally he told the others to go on."

Suzannah imagined herself snowed in alone up high in the mountains. "I wouldn't want to stay behind!"

"Mose didn't like it, either. He said he never felt so lonely in all his life as when his two friends disappeared into all that whiteness. But there was nothing else to do. After they left, he tried trapping, but the best he could catch was a fox or two and sometimes a half-starved coyote."

"He—he lived, didn't he?"

"He lived. That's how we know what happened that fall. Three months later, a man from their party came back for him. He made better snowshoes for Mose and showed him how to use them, and the next morning, they set out on the trail and somehow got through."

"Where did you hear about this?" Suzannah asked.

"At Fort Hall."

"Then, if it's so dangerous, why did Uncle Franklin want us to go to California? Why didn't we just keep on for Oregon?"

Daniel drew a deep breath. "Don't you remember?

It's because he thinks it's important to keep the family together. And after Charles heard about the gold strike in California, he was halfway there!"

*Charles again!* Suzannah thought with a rush of anger.

She glanced at her sister sitting in the wagon. "Don't tell *her* about the blizzard of '44."

"I won't," Daniel said. "Guess I shouldn't have told you, either, but I figured you ought to know how important it is to keep moving no matter how hard things get."

Suzannah eyed the soaring snow-capped mountains that loomed ahead, and shivered a little. What was around the next bend on that narrow, winding trail?

The path twisted and turned like the sidewinder she had almost stepped on once down on the prairie. And it was every bit as dangerous! In places, the trail was so narrow that the oxen's hooves came right to the edge and broke off chunks of rock that tumbled over the side, down, down, down to the ravine below.

Suzannah's prayer each day was very much the same: *Lord, please don't let the oxen break through and fall into the canyons . . . and help Pauline get through this.*

At one especially steep incline, Suzannah told her sister, "You'll have to get out of the wagon with Jamie."

Pauline clutched the little boy and stared at her in horror. She had always been afraid of heights.

When Uncle Franklin saw her panic, he was quick to say, "Maybe they're better off in the wagon than walking beside these cliffs."

"You're probably right," Suzannah agreed. "I'm scared myself."

"If the truth were known, I imagine everyone is

scared," Uncle Franklin said. "We just have to move on, one step at a time. It's like walking with God."

Uncle Franklin and Daniel led the oxen up the steep incline, while Pauline peered out, white-faced.

"Don't look, Pauline!" Suzannah called.

Her sister's eyes were open, but Suzannah had a feeling that Pauline saw nothing.

Loose rock rolled out from under the wagon, but, slowly and steadily, the oxen pulled the wagon up the incline. Then the next wagon fell in behind and repeated the slow process. One by one, each team followed suit until all of them were safely across the difficult stretch of trail.

Finally Captain Monroe, his beard blown back in the brisk breeze, rode by with instructions. "Here comes our hunting party. We'll stop early to eat since we expect even rougher climbing this afternoon."

*Rougher climbing?* Suzannah wondered whether Pauline could hold on one more time.

Just then, Uncle Karl and Cousin Garth rode in with the hunting party. Lately, they'd been bringing in rabbits, but today a deer was tied to Uncle Karl's horse. "We won't starve yet," he said as he slid off his horse.

Suzannah noticed that no one laughed. They had no other food, not unless they killed the oxen—and they needed them to get over the mountains.

"There better be some gold left in California after all we've been through to get there!" Uncle Karl stated as he began to untie the deer.

Garth helped him carry the animal over to the side, and they made quick work of gutting and cleaning it. The others helped feed and water the oxen, left standing in their tracks on the trail.

"S'pose it might all be gone by now?" Garth asked his father.

Uncle Karl shrugged. But Suzannah saw that the

question bothered the others as much as it bothered her. What if there was no gold left when they reached California?

Suzannah refused to think that way. Instead, she asked the others, "What would you do if you struck it rich?"

"I'd buy myself a mansion and live like a king," said Mr. Murphy.

"And I'd buy hundreds of new dresses, one for every day of the year, and bonnets to match, and some red shoes—" Bridgette Murphy decided.

Suzannah gave a wry glance at her own faded frock. "Guess I could use some new dresses, too," she told Daniel. "But not *hundreds!* After that—and plenty of food—I'd just want to get settled in a house and stay put. How about you?"

"Same here," he agreed. "Except . . . on the frontier, they'll be needing churches and schools for the people moving in. So I'd want to use some of the gold to help build 'em."

Suzannah gave Daniel a sidelong look. He was dead serious. Funny, how her cousin never thought of himself first. She wished Charles could be like that!

When the dinner gong sounded at last, Aunt Ruthie looked Pauline over and whispered to Suzannah, "Your sister's feeling puny again. Your Uncle Franklin and I can't do anything with her, but maybe you can. Make sure she eats, since she's eating for *two* now."

So she *had* noticed, Suzannah thought, studying Pauline's rounded front that not even her shapeless pinafore could hide now. "I'm not sure she'll listen to me, either," she told Aunt Ruthie. "But I'll try."

Later, when she carried the stew to the wagon, Jamie grabbed for it. "Eat!" he crowed happily.

"You mustn't let him eat everything," Suzannah told

her sister. "You've got to keep up your strength for the baby's sake—" She swallowed hard, forcing herself to say something nice about her brother-in-law—"and for Charles. When we're through these mountains, you'll all be together again."

"Yes." Pauline brightened. "We'll be together."

"You don't want Charles to see you so spindly and sick, do you?"

Pauline shook her head and choked down a few more bites.

"If he sees you looking like this, he'll say, 'What's happened to my beautiful wife?' "

Pauline flushed and began to eat more heartily than she had in days.

Every day thereafter, when they stopped to eat, Suzannah took pains to remind Pauline what Charles would say if she neglected her appearance. Nagging her sister made her feel a little guilty.

But when it snowed one night, Suzannah thought of Mose Schallenberger. If he, a strong young boy, had had trouble staying up on snowshoes, what would happen to Pauline if she got any weaker? As for Jamie, he was too heavy to carry for long. *Lord, help us all!* she prayed.

By morning, the snow had melted. But the mountain trail was too steep and muddy for the oxen to manage. Every step took them dangerously close to the edge. Suzannah helped Daniel lead the team slowly and carefully, but she cringed when their hooves struck the rim of the cliff, sending loose rock and gravel echoing down the mountainside.

Finally, Mordechai gave new orders. "Empty them wagons and double-team the oxen!" he barked. "With ten

or twelve oxen pullin' a wagon, we kin make it. When we
git to the top, ye kin carry yer belongin's up and reload
'em. But ye might as well face it—ye won't be makin'
much progress in the next few weeks."

The emigrants moaned.

"So this is why Mose Schallenberger's party was here
in the mountains so late," Suzannah said.

"Shhh!" he hushed her. "Pauline's listening."

Suzannah spoke to her sister as gently as possible.
"We have to unload the wagon now, Pauline."

Pauline stared at her with vacant eyes.

"Pauline—" Suzannah pleaded. "Please, Pauline, we
have to unpack the wagon. It's too heavy for the oxen to
pull up this steep hill. We're the second in line now, and
we don't want to hold up all the others."

Pauline shook her head. Strands of long blond hair
had come loose from the bun at the back of her neck and
straggled over her shoulders. She looked like a wild woman
as she shook her head harder and harder.

"Never mind," Suzannah said, patting her arm.
"Daniel and I will do it."

Soon trunks, churn, quilts, lanterns, mattress, grub
box, and other belongings were piled beside the granite
wall of the mountain. In front, some of the men were busily
hitching four more oxen to Uncle Franklin's wagon, the
first in line.

It was one thing to have heard Mordechai tell about
it, but another for Suzannah to see the team of ten oxen
pulling Uncle Franklin's wagon over the ridge.

She looked away in dread. "Come on, Pauline. You
have to get out of the wagon now. We're next."

Pauline shook her head again.

"I'll carry Jamie," Aunt Ruthie offered.

Pauline handed him down to her.

"Now it's your turn, Pauline," Suzannah said encouragingly.

"No!" Pauline protested, her eyes bright with tears. "I won't get out! I *can't!*"

"It's going to take ten oxen to pull the wagon over that ridge, Pauline. You can't stay in here."

"I won't get out!" her sister said, tears streaming down her cheeks.

Hearing the commotion, Mordechai hurried over. "Miz Herrin'ton, ye've got to git out. It's dangerous."

Pauline didn't answer.

Suzannah climbed up into the wagon. "Pauline—"

Suddenly Pauline caught hold of her with a terrifying grip. "Stay with me, Suzannah!" she wailed. "Please, please stay with me!"

Suzannah glanced out at the others. Aunt Ruthie and Aunt Pearl were appalled.

"Be reasonable, Pauline," Aunt Ruthie pleaded. "You can't stay in the wagon and neither can Suzannah. Come on down here now. It's frightening for all of us, dear, but you're only making yourself ill."

Pauline only gripped Suzannah more tightly. Finally Suzannah knew what had to be done.

"I'll stay with her," she said. "We'll sit in the front of the wagon bed and hold onto the driver's seat."

Mordechai shrugged his thin shoulders, his white beard flying in the chill breeze. "If thet's the way ye want it, thet's the way it'll have t' be, I reckon. But I'm tellin' ye, ye'll be riskin' life and limb."

Pauline still wouldn't budge, so Suzannah eased herself and her sister to the floor of the wagon bed. "Throw us two ropes," she told Daniel, trying to hide her own fear. "I'll tie us to the wagon the best I can."

Daniel threw in the ropes, and Suzannah wound them around Pauline and then herself, tying each of them to the seat. If the wagon bounced over the slabs of granite, it would be better to be tied in than to be thrown over the ridge into the canyon.

At last the extra oxen were in place in front of the wagon, and Mordechai yelled, "Wagons, ho!" Daniel joined the others in urging the oxen up the steeply tilted slabs of stone.

The wagon lurched forward, and Suzannah clutched her sister with one hand and the wagon with the other. She gazed up at the ten oxen straining in front of them and at the mountain peaks silhouetted against the blue sky. Above the rattling of the harnesses and the creak of wagon wheels, she quoted a psalm, loud enough for Pauline to hear every word: "The Lord is my shepherd; I shall not want. He maketh me to lie down in green pastures; he leadeth me beside the still waters. He restoreth my soul. . . . Yea, though I walk through the valley of the shadow of death I will fear no evil: for thou art with me—"

Slowly her fear and her anger with Pauline drained away, and she knew that, whatever happened, they were in God's hands.

"If Mother were here, she'd say we must have faith in God, even when we're in the valley of the shadow of death," Suzannah said. "Let's sing 'Fairest Lord Jesus' like we used to at church in Alexandria. Close your eyes, Pauline, and pretend we're still there."

Suzannah began singing:

*Fairest Lord Jesus, Ruler of all nature,*
*O Thou of God and man the Son. . . .*

Pauline's eyes were closed, but now her lips opened and her voice came in a whisper,

*Thee will I cherish, Thee will I honor,*
*Thou, my soul's Glory, Joy, and Crown.*

Suzannah sang on and Pauline with her, her voice gaining power:

*Fair are the meadows, fairer still the woodlands,*
*Robed in the blooming garb of spring,*
*Jesus is fairer, Jesus is purer,*
*Who makes the woeful heart to sing.*

It occurred to Suzannah as the wagon bumped up the ridge that this might be the first time anyone had ever sung this hymn in these mountains, so she sang with all of her might as Pauline's voice gathered to its full strength:

*Fair is the sunshine, fairer still the moonlight,*
*And all the twinkling, starry host:*
*Jesus shines brighter, Jesus shines purer,*
*Than all the angels heaven can boast.*

When Pauline's blue eyes opened and turned to her, they were filled with light and joy. Suddenly it didn't matter if they ever made it up the mountain in this rickety covered wagon still climbing skyward, or through fierce snowstorms, or even down the other side of the mountains. For in this moment, God had transformed Pauline into her old self again.

# CHAPTER FIVE

"There's one good thing 'bout this mountain climb," Mordechai said one day as he led his spotted pony by the line of covered wagons. "We left them Injuns behind."

"It's even too awful here for them," Suzannah answered. She looked more closely into his face. "Looks to me like you still have bad news."

Mordechai nodded. "Got to watch for grizzly bear all around this forest. We been seein' their tracks today."

"Grizzly bears?" Suzannah repeated.

"Biggest, most powerful bear in the world," Mordechai replied. "They'll send a man flyin' with one swipe of a paw."

Suzannah didn't quite believe him. "Is that so? Well, a mother bear and two cubs chased us down the National Road in Ohio . . . but we outran them."

Mordechai gave a snort. "Them Eastern bears ain't more'n cubs to the Western grizzlies. Best to watch out fer 'em . . . and keep yer dogs away from 'em, too," he warned. Then he moved on.

Suzannah's eyes met Daniel's. "Mordechai seems full of gloomy news," she said.

"It's part of his job to warn us of dangers."

"I suppose so, but I don't like it."

"At least the forests here are beautiful," Daniel said, looking at the evergreen trees all around them. "Have you ever seen such huge pines?"

"And they're spaced far enough apart so the wagons can wind through them," Suzannah observed. "But now I'm expecting to see a grizzly in every tree!"

"Grizzlies don't climb trees," Daniel said. "They aren't like the black bears back East."

Suzannah drew a breath. "Just more dangerous!"

After a while, Suzannah glanced back to see Pauline climbing from the back of the wagon onto the driver's seat, sketchbook in hand.

"Look, Daniel. Pauline's sketching again. And we've been praying together every morning and night since that awful day on the ridge."

"Goes to prove we shouldn't give up on anyone," he said. "The Lord never does."

As they walked along, a deer flitted through the trees on the other side of the wagon.

"A deer!" Suzannah whispered.

Moments later, her heart almost stopped. Behind a nearby pine tree, a great bear stood watching the deer leaping through the underbrush. The brownish-yellow beast rose up on its hind legs, sniffing the air, its massive head turned away from the wagons rumbling along the trail.

"A grizzly! That's why the deer was running!"

Keeping his pony to a walk, Mordechai rode up at that moment, rifle in hand.

"Daniel, git out yer rifle," he said quietly, "but don't shoot if ye don't have to. Bullets don't always stop a grizzly."

From the wagon, Pauline had seen the bear, too. She stifled a scream with a shaking hand.

"Suzannah, git into the wagon with your sister," Mordechai ordered. "If the bear comes fer the oxen, stay there and don't git out no matter what."

Suzannah climbed aboard the wagon and held her sister. In the wagons ahead, Uncle Franklin, Uncle Karl, and Garth loaded their rifles. Aunt Pearl tugged Lad and Lass into her wagon, clamping their muzzles shut with her hands to keep them from barking, while the mothers shushed small children and pulled them into the wagons.

Catching their scent as the wind shifted, the bear turned its head in their direction.

"Keep movin' along, natural-like," Mordechai murmured.

Suzannah kept her eyes fixed on the bear. Every creak of the wagon and clang of the iron-rimmed wheels against the rocks sounded hideously loud to her. Surely the grizzly would come for them. But Mordechai had said to keep moving—

The bear watched them move along the trail. For an instant, she felt as if their eyes met and locked. Horrified, she sent up a quick prayer: *Please help us, Lord! And the wagons behind us . . . and Ned in back with the livestock.*

To her amazement, the bear only watched them pass by, then turned away and disappeared into the forest.

"A grizzly would rather run than fight, unless ye git 'im cornered or it's a mother grizzly with cubs," Mordechai said. "Could be we're the first humans this'un's ever seen."

Suzannah felt grateful when the entire wagon train, including Ned and the loose livestock, was far beyond the grassy glade. But she kept her eyes open for the rest of the grizzly's family.

That evening, they stood on the shore of a beautiful blue lake and looked ahead at a towering mountain pass.

One of the emigrants hollered over to Mordechai, "Don't tell us we have to climb that pass!"

"Ain't no other way I know to git acrost it," he muttered as he rode past.

The sun was sinking fast now, and the mountains gleamed with a fierce light.

"It looks like the pot of gold at the end of the rainbow!" Suzannah cried, thinking again what lay just beyond those mountains. If they could find gold, she and Pauline could have a real home for Jamie and the new baby, and they'd never have to move again.

"But I don't like the looks of those dark clouds moving over the pass," Daniel remarked.

"Snow clouds?" Again Suzannah remembered the story of Mose Schallenberger, who had been trapped by a blizzard just four years ago. "Isn't it too early for snow?"

Daniel only shrugged. "Guess we'll find out."

By morning, Mordechai had scouted the next few miles and rode back to camp with the news. He pointed to the range of mountains before them. "Ain't more'n two days' travel, but we'll be lucky to make it in five. The hardest part of the journey's still ahead."

"You never have anything but bad news for us," grumbled Suzannah. But if Mordechai heard her, he paid no attention and rode on.

Even in her warmest dress and cloak, Suzannah was

shivering. "It's getting colder and colder. Time to change into my boots," she said.

When she climbed into the wagon and pulled them on, she found the boots much tighter than she remembered. "I can't believe I wore them just four months ago," she told Pauline.

"It's from walking in those moccasins all this time," her sister replied. "You're going to have big feet, Suzannah Colton! Not only that, you're going to look like an Indian yourself if you don't start wearing your sunbonnet! Mother would have a fit if she could see you."

"You know what, Pauline? You're beginning to sound more and more like your old self."

Pauline smiled. "Well, you've given me plenty of reason to worry."

"I worry about you, too—riding in the wagon when there's danger of you and Jamie falling out—"

"I can't carry Jamie anymore," Pauline sighed, looking down at her expanding waistline. "He's just getting too heavy for me."

Suzannah nodded. "Well, I hope this satisfies you, at least. I'm putting my sunbonnet up. Now where are my muffler, mittens, and sweater?"

Pauline dug them out of the trunk for her. "Aunt Ruthie insisted we take one of her buffalo robes to use at night now. Mordechai says that up in the pass, it'll be even colder than Virginia winters!"

Suzannah shivered again. "Then I'll wear my old cap *under* my sunbonnet. That should please you."

Pauline smiled. "Even Mother would be pleased! Remember how she used to say, 'Bundle up, girls, it's cold outside'?"

Suzannah climbed down from the wagon. What *would* Mother and Father think of them being on this journey—

fording rivers, climbing mountains, staring down a grizzly
bear, and now facing this terrible mountain pass?

"There's a thin layer of ice on the water buckets!"
Aunt Ruthie called out the next morning when she went
out to make coffee for breakfast.

Suzannah didn't like the idea of it, nor the sight of the
heavy clouds hovering over the mountains. Even when the
sun broke through, there was a wintry chill in the air.

For three days they struggled to keep the wagons
moving to the top of the pass. And Mordechai pulled out
every trick he knew to keep the wagons rolling, all the
while keeping an eye out for grizzlies.

"Empty them wagons!" he would yell. "Double-team
them oxen!" "Rope 'em to the trees 'n pull!"

A light snow was falling just before they reached the
top, and everyone layered on even more clothing, making it
harder to trudge along through the pass.

"Keep goin'—" Mordechai warned. "Got to keep
goin' no matter how tired ye git."

The thick fluffy white snow clung to every pine needle
and shrub. And still it came down—feather-light and
soft—shutting out the jagged peaks.

By midday, the whole world around them was white.
And by nightfall, when they stopped to make camp, they
could hardly see the wagon in front of them.

When the hunting party returned, Uncle Karl said,
"The animals are smarter'n we are. They've moved on
down to forage for food. I expect even the grizzlies are
hibernatin'."

"At least we can melt snow for water and add it to our
soup," Suzannah said.

But the snow came down so heavily that it was hard

to keep a campfire going, even with Daniel and Garth holding up an India rubber tent to block the snow. After trying for a while, Uncle Franklin said, "We'll have to eat cold soup and biscuits in our wagons."

Suzannah and Pauline filled bowls for themselves and Jamie and tied the wagon's canvas cover tight against the cold. And later, Suzannah was glad for Aunt Pearl's buffalo blanket over them, and extra quilts beneath.

When she awoke during the night, there was only a strange stillness outside. She strained to hear. Was it still snowing? She pulled the buffalo blanket over her head.

The next morning, when she cracked open the front flap of the canvas and peered out, she was struck dumb to see how much it had snowed. "The snow has stopped," she told Pauline, her breath coming in white puffs. "But—"

"But what?" Pauline pushed herself up in the make-shift bed, hugging the blanket to her.

"But it's ... awfully cold," Suzannah finished, deciding not to break the news to her sister just yet.

Thick mounds of snow covered every visible surface. Not three feet of it, like the storm that had trapped Mose Schallenberger, but a fearful lot.

Spotting the dogs frisking about outside, she chose a safer topic of conversation. "Lad and Lass seem to like it. And Daniel and Uncle Franklin have a cookfire going. Looks like they're thawing the ice and making coffee."

"Mmmmmm. I thought I smelled coffee," Pauline said as she put Jamie's mittens on him. "Since it's so cold, you can try a cup. I doubt that just a little would stunt your growth. Don't give Jamie any, though. Best if he just drinks hot water."

"Brrrr," Jamie said. "Cold."

Suzannah climbed down from the wagon and stepped into snow up to her shoe tops. Almost a foot of snow, she guessed. Slowly she made her way to the back of the wagon to get the tin cups and plates from their grub box.

Ducking her head into the biting wind, Suzannah struggled through the snow to the cookfire. Putting out her mittened hands to its warmth, she told Aunt Ruthie what Pauline had said about the coffee.

"Oh, I don't think it would hurt for a few days. But I do wish we had hot chocolate for you and Jamie. Or at least a little milk to cut the coffee's strength."

Suzannah held out her tin mug as Aunt Ruthie poured the steaming hot liquid. The steam felt good to her face as she bent her head over the cup, holding it with both hands to warm her fingers. When the coffee had cooled a little, she tried a sip. Bitter, but hot. She took another sip, wondering what grown-ups thought was so all-fired delicious about the stuff.

"Sorry we don't have anything for breakfast except some dried beef. But we'll make a little broth and that should keep up our strength for a while."

Though they cooked the dried beef as long as possible, it was still tough. As far as Suzannah was concerned, the only good thing about dried beef was its salty broth, which tasted a lot better than coffee.

Retracing her steps to the wagon, Suzannah carefully carried two cups for Pauline and Jamie. And soon, Mordechai's shrill voice brought their skimpy breakfast to an end.

"Catch up! Catch up yer oxen!"

Suzannah rushed to help Daniel yoke and hitch their oxen to the wagon. While they were working, a lazy snowflake drifted to the ground. And then another. By the time they had finished rigging the oxen, a heavy snow was falling again.

Before Daniel could complain, Suzannah said, "We

ought to celebrate. Some days I didn't think we'd ever make it to the top of this mountain!"

Through his heavy wool muffler, her cousin managed a half-hearted "Hurray!"

But that wasn't good enough for Suzannah. "Hurray!" she shouted to the top of her lungs, listening for the echo that came from the surrounding canyons. "We made it! Hurray!"

Mordechai, looking like a little old snowman as he rode by on No-Name, put a damper on her enthusiasm. "Too soon for celebratin'. Now we've got to git down this here mountain. It ain't easy, either."

Mordechai was right. On the western slope of the mountains, the going was even rougher. Now there was the added danger of broken axles and runaway oxen on the steep downgrade.

Nor did the snowstorm let up. The driving snow made it almost impossible to stay on the trail.

"Tie those wagons to the trees!" their old guide would shout. "Now let 'er down . . . little by little . . . not so fast or thet wagon will break up! Watch them icy spots—"

One morning, when the oxen were lumbering down the path, their hooves hit a patch of ice. Before anyone could stop them, they were skidding down the slope, the wagon bouncing wildly behind them.

Suzannah's heart pounded as she slipped and slid, following them down the slope. *What if Pauline and her baby and Jamie are . . . hurt?* she thought. She dared not think past that awful possibility.

Ahead, the lead oxen finally came to a stop, their yokes wedged against the trunk of a pine tree, the wagon amazingly upright. The oxen, though, were on their knees,

bawling, and Suzannah felt like bawling, too, as she skidded into them and fell. Beside her, Lad and Lass yipped with terror.

Just then Pauline and Jamie stuck their heads out of the wagon. "We're fine, praise God!" Pauline said. "Shaky and probably a little bruised, but alive!"

Suzannah took a deep breath and let it out slowly. "You're sure?"

"Absolutely!" Pauline insisted, then put her hands over her swollen stomach. "In fact, we're *all* fine."

With Lad and Lass jumping up to lick the snow off her face, Suzannah picked herself up and dusted herself off.

Behind them, Mordechai reined in his pony. "Don't let them oxen slide downhill like thet!" he scolded. "Do ye want 'em to break their legs?"

"How could we have stopped them?" Suzannah asked. With visions of Rose and Iris, who had broken their legs in the Forty-Mile Desert and had to be shot, she pulled aside a snowy pine bough and examined the animals.

"You all right, boys?" Amazingly, they weren't cut or bleeding.

"Maybe they're just scared," Daniel said when he reached her.

The two of them tugged the animals to their feet, and the oxen finally quietened.

"Try your legs," she urged, pulling them forward.

Slowly, very slowly, they began to plow through the snow again. "Good, boys . . . good boys—"

"They're all right!" She waved to Mordechai on the trail above them. "No harm done!"

He probably thought she and Daniel had been careless, but she didn't see how anyone could have prevented what had happened here. And even at that, they had been lucky. Or was it luck? Surely once again the Lord had been watching over them.

The next day, the going grew even worse. A howling wind blasted snow at them, and they pulled down their caps and covered their faces with their mufflers until only their eyes peeked out.

Since the wagons could make only very slow progress, there was less danger of runaways, and Suzannah grew tired of pushing her way through the snow. Narrowing her eyes against the blowing snow, Suzannah spied a square of logs jutting from the snow, well back from the trail.

"Let's see what it is!" she called to Daniel, leaving the wagon train to explore.

Reaching a cluster of pine trees, she stopped to catch her breath. After a moment, she ventured toward the log formation.

"Coming?" she shouted back to Daniel.

Her cousin's answer disappeared into his muffler and the driving wind, so she trudged on alone.

"A chimney?" she wondered as she neared the place where she had seen the logs. *Yes, it was a chimney sticking out of the snow.*

The fresh snow near the chimney had not packed down, and her feet sank in deeper with each step. "It's an abandoned cabin," Suzannah called back, sinking in deeper still.

Suddenly her feet struck something solid, and she began sliding downward. "Help! I'm slipping!"

At that moment Daniel appeared. "Suzannah! Catch this!" he yelled, flinging his bullwhip out to her.

Miraculously she caught it, slowing her icy plunge.

"Hold on!" Daniel shouted into the wind.

She gripped the end of the bullwhip with all of her might. Now she knew what had happened. A cabin was buried in the snow beneath her, and she had been sliding down the roof! If she couldn't hold onto the whip, she was in danger of breaking through the snow and sliding all the way to the ground below. If so, she would be buried with the cabin!

Daniel pulled hard on the whip. Little by little, she edged her way out of the deep snow and away from the treacherous ledge. Slowly she made her way over to the pine trees where the snow was not so deep.

Catching sight of them, Mordechai left the wagon train and helped them struggle back to the trail.

"Don't ye ever git off the trail agin!" he warned, when they were safe. "There's deep gullies hereabouts!"

When Suzannah finally caught her breath, she asked, "Was that Mose Schallenberger's cabin?"

Mordechai gave a curt nod. "Ye know the story?"

"We know it," Daniel replied.

"Well, if ye don't stay out of trouble, ye'll end up like him! Now let's git goin' afore the others are out of sight."

Day by day they battled the snow, working their way down along forested ridges, up and down canyons, and into the foothills. Mordechai had said it would take two months from the Raft River to reach the California gold fields. Well, it was October 7, exactly two months since they had left the river, and the gold fields of California were nowhere in sight.

When it finally stopped snowing and the sky cleared, Suzannah stared with amazement. "Look, Daniel, at the valley! A great valley . . . with no snow!"

"It must be the Sacramento Valley," Daniel said. "We must be near the gold fields!"

"That's jest where we are," Mordechai said. "Ye've come two thousand miles from Missouri—maybe even more, what with all the ziggin' 'n zaggin' along rivers and through mountains. When I first laid eyes on ye, I had my doubts ye'd make it."

"Two thousand miles!" the emigrants shouted.

Suzannah's heart leapt with joy and thanksgiving. "And we've come even farther—all the way from Virginia!"

"Praise the Lord!" said Aunt Ruthie. "He's answered our prayers."

Uncle Franklin let out a deep breath. "No more Indian alarms, no more buffalo stampedes, no more pulling, carrying, and hauling wagons! We might be tired and ragged, but we made it!"

A sweet smile lit Pauline's face, and despite her exhaustion, Suzannah thought her sister looked younger and prettier than she had seen her in a long time. "Just think!" exclaimed Pauline joyously. "Charles is somewhere in these foothills!"

*So are grizzly bears,* was Suzannah's first thought. But she decided not to voice her opinion, nor to let her brother-in-law trouble her now. "We're here!" she yelled. "We made it to California!"

And in her heart, she remembered to thank the One who had brought them safely across the high mountains.

# CHAPTER SIX

Early in the week, the wagon train began its slow descent through forested foothills and golden valleys, lush with groves of live oak trees. "It looks just like the kind of place where you'd find gold!" Suzannah said happily. "After all we've been through, let's hope we find *lots* of it!"

"And let's hope you won't be disappointed," Uncle Franklin cautioned. "Most gold rushes don't last long."

"Besides, we're here to find Charles so we can be a complete family again," Aunt Ruthie reminded her.

Charles was the last person in the world Suzannah wanted to think about. More and more often in the past few weeks, she had whiled away the long hours by pondering what she would do when she found gold. She'd need a lot of it to take care of Pauline, Jamie, and the baby, in case Charles didn't show up.

Mordechai, who had ridden ahead, now had returned with two bearded miners to guide them to Coloma. "They's plenty of gold to be found!" he told the emigrants. "It's all over these here mountains!"

Suzannah quivered with excitement.

"In some places ya can pick it up right off the ground," said one red-shirted miner. "In others, where the rivers and streams have washed the gold along, ya might find it under rocks and tree roots. The Injuns have always said, 'Heavy yellow rock, bad medicine,' so they've stayed away from it till now. That's why it's all still here!"

"We'll be rich in no time!" Mr. Murphy exclaimed.

"Lord," Uncle Franklin prayed under his breath, "keep us from greed and temptation."

"But if God's put the gold here, why shouldn't we find it?" Suzannah wanted to know.

"It's not gold itself that's bad," Uncle Franklin explained, "but the possibility of loving it more than God. He warns us not to put any idols before Him, and gold, like anything else, can become an idol."

The blue-shirted miner nodded. "Gold fever," he said. "Most everybody's got it. Worst of all, there's thousands of miners now. Shiploads of 'em from Oregon, Chile, the Sandwich Islands, even China! And I hear tell that the Sonorans are marchin' up from Mexico. Everybody wants to git in on the gold rush."

"What does the gold look like when you find it?" asked Captain Monroe.

The red-shirted miner took a pouch from his pocket and shook the gold out into his hand. "Here 'tis!"

Suzannah crowded around with the other emigrants to see it.

"This here's a nugget," he said, pointing out a piece as big as a walnut. "They always feel heavy for their size. These here that look like fish scales are called flakes. And these tiny seedlike bits or this dust ain't worth much unless you get enough of it."

"We heerd of nuggets the size o' *potatoes,*" someone complained.

"Ain't too many of *them,*" the miner said. "But I did see a five-pound chunk."

"There's talk of a thick vein where you kin jest cut off as much as you want, like cuttin' a chunk of sourdough bread off the end of a loaf," said the other miner.

The red-shirted miner grinned. "But we ain't seen it yet, and believe me, we've been lookin'."

"That's just what I'd like . . . a thick vein of gold where I can cut off as much as I want," Suzannah said.

Garth laughed. "I doubt they'd even allow girls in the gold fields. That's man's work."

She squared her shoulders. "We'll see about that!" Hadn't she been doing the work of a man, helping Daniel bullwhack oxen all the way across the mountains, and taking care of her sister and nephew?

"Well, if ye find gold," began the blue-shirted miner, "don't make a noise of it, or ye'll have hunderds of miners diggin' out your spot. Don't even let on to yer best friend. The news always gits out, and ye'll git crowded out of yer own diggin's."

Suzannah decided right then and there that if she ever found gold, she'd keep it a secret. She wouldn't even tell Daniel or Uncle Franklin. But she'd be sure to do something wonderful for all of them with it.

"I'll guide ye on to Coloma where the first gold was found," Mordechai told the emigrants. "Then I'll count my guidin' work done. I mean to find gold myself."

"You tired of guidin' greenhorns?" Uncle Karl asked.

"Ye said it, not me!" Mordechai protested with a grin, and everyone burst into laughter.

"Can't say I blame him," Suzannah told Daniel.

"You couldn't get me to go over that trail again for all the gold in the world. It's a miracle we made it!"

At their nooning stop, the miners answered the emigrants' questions about James Marshall discovering the first gold by a sawmill on the American River.

"But thet was jest the beginnin'," the red-shirted miner said. "Ye kin find gold layin' on the ground or in the riverbeds or under the rock layers. Sometimes big chunks of it. Some miners claim it comes from the devil's blowhole in the middle of the earth."

"A professor here in the diggin's says it was flung out of the mountains by volcanoes," put in the blue-shirted miner. "That's why, in the beginnin', there was so much to be found just layin' about."

"Devil's blowhole or volcanoes, I don't care how it got there!" Suzannah told Daniel. "I plan to find all I can!"

Her cousin gave her a long look. "Sounds like you've got a touch of gold fever already."

"Not me," she protested. "I'll just find enough gold to build Pauline and me a house and get settled, and then I'll stop."

"What about Charles?"

"I'll cross that bridge when I come to it. We may never even see him again."

"I've had that thought myself."

"I wonder if Pauline has," Suzannah said. "It's a worry to me about—" She almost gave away Pauline's secret, but stopped in time.

Daniel's green eyes met hers, and she quickly added, "I *have* to find gold. No matter what happens, I don't want to live under Charles's thumb forever."

That afternoon they rode down a ravine and found tents lining the banks of a stream. Hundreds of men were hard at work with pickaxes and shovels. Some stood knee-

deep in the streams, swirling the water and gravel in metal and wooden pans—panning gold.

Looking up from their work, some of the miners stopped to stare at them, and Suzannah told Daniel, "They're all men. Not a girl or a woman among them."

"I tried to tell you."

After a moment, she said, "I thought we were going to find gold lying on top of the ground."

"So did I," Mr. Murphy said, disappointed. "I didn't count on doin' no diggin'. Where's the hotels?" he yelled across the ditch to two miners working nearby.

The men straightened up from their digging and roared with laughter. "Out yonder under the trees. Most of us bunk in our bedrolls. With yer wagons, yer better off than most."

"Oh, no! Looks like we're still going to have to live in our wagons," Suzannah moaned to Aunt Ruthie.

"Let's not jump to conclusions," her aunt suggested. "And let's count our blessings."

"After all we've endured, I'd rather count *gold*," Suzannah grumbled, then felt ashamed of herself.

Pauline sat in the wagon, scanning the miners' faces. "Do any of you know my husband, Charles Herrington?" she called out.

They looked her over, taking in little Jamie, who was trying to get down to dig in the dirt. Ragged as they were, Pauline still looked like a lady.

"Don't believe we do, ma'am," said one miner. Then he turned away and got back to his digging.

A little farther on along the stream, she called down again, "Do you know my husband . . . Charles Herrington from Virginia?"

Again, the men eyed her, then shook their heads.

"I believe they've heard of him all right, but they aren't about to tell Pauline," Suzannah muttered to Daniel.

As they traveled along toward Coloma, Uncle Franklin asked a miner, "Any sign of a Virginia man named Charles Herrington?"

"Gambler?" the man asked. "A dark, handsome fella?"

Uncle Franklin nodded. "That he is."

"Just around the bend a mile or so." The miner pointed a grimy finger. "He owns the gamblin' tent in the tent town near the next gulch."

Suzannah didn't like the sound of it. Not one bit.

As they walked along beside the wagons, winding their way through the field crowded with miners at work, Uncle Franklin and Uncle Karl talked together quietly.

They eyed their surroundings with distaste until the wagon train came upon an isolated clearing, bordered by a stream and shade trees and located under an overhanging cliff.

"Why hasn't anyone camped here?" Uncle Franklin asked.

"Dry diggin's, I expect," said the red-shirted miner. "Probably no gold in the stream."

"It looks like a fine place for a family to set up camp," Uncle Franklin said. "We don't want to live among miners, not with our women and children along."

Suzannah inspected their surroundings. The sheer cliff curved around, forming a large sheltered space covered with grasses, boulders, and a few tall trees. The stream, carving a path through the front of the clearing, ran closer to the road and was marked by large boulders near its banks.

Across the dusty road, almost hidden by oak, cedar, and pine trees, stood a rustic settlement. Five log cabins had been built far back in the wooded area. Suzannah was curious about who might live there.

The uncles conferred with Aunt Ruthie and Aunt Pearl for a few minutes. And moments later, when Mordechai rode along on No-Name, Uncle Franklin hailed him. "We'll be leaving you here. We want to thank you for guiding us safely."

Mordechai raised his brows in surprise. "Ye won't be goin' on to Coloma with us?"

"Karl figures it's probably picked clean by now, like the hunting grounds at the jumping off place," Uncle Franklin explained. "This looks like a good spot for now, since we hear Charles is over at the next gulch."

Mordechai rubbed his chin through his wispy white beard. "I'm aimin' to look elsewhere myself, but I promised to take the wagon train all the way to Coloma."

"That's because yer a man of yer word," said Uncle Karl.

"Try to be," Mordechai replied, then grinned broadly. "Been a pleasure to know yer family. Kind'a wish now thet I'd a settled down with one myself."

Uncle Franklin and Uncle Karl shook hands with him, and Suzannah hurried over to give Mordechai a hug. But the old man backed off and stuck out his hand instead.

"Knowed ye'd make a right fine bullwhacker," he said. "As good as any I've seed . . . better'n some."

Her eyes misted over. "And I think you're the best guide in the whole wild West! Thank you, Mordechai . . . thank you for everything!"

All of a sudden, Captain Monroe and the rest of the emigrants were bidding them farewell. Even Ned was leaving.

"I'm goin' down to Coloma," he told Daniel, "just to see it. If you're still around these parts, I'll find you when I come back."

He gave Suzannah a long look, and she wondered if he was going to Coloma to be near Bridgette.

Before the wagon train had disappeared around the hillside, Uncle Franklin had set the family in motion.

"First, let's get the wagons situated under those cedar trees toward the back, but not too near the cliff in case of a rockslide. Boys," he instructed, "you water the horses and oxen. Then, while you ladies tend to the housekeeping chores, Karl and I will ride on to find Charles and see about buying provisions."

"Do you suppose there's a place to buy some calico and flannel?" asked Aunt Ruthie. "Our clothes are in shreds, and we've traded or used up all the fabric we brought with us."

"Done," Uncle Franklin said. "If we can find some kind of general store, that is."

"Can you get us some fruit and vegetables?" Aunt Pearl asked Uncle Karl. "It's been so long since any of us have had any."

"That might take some doin'," Uncle Karl said, "but we'll try our best."

The idea of staying in one place for a while spurred them all to action.

"That's a natural corral made of boulders back by the cliff," Daniel told Garth. "There's even green grass for the livestock. We'd just need to make a gate."

"Could build one out of saplings," Uncle Karl said.

They pulled the wagons under the huge cedar trees in no time, and Uncle Franklin and Uncle Karl were soon riding off on their horses. Garth took the oxen and dogs to the stream to drink, and Daniel set about chopping down saplings to use for the corral gate.

While Jamie napped in the wagon, Pauline got out and stretched. "Seems like a good time to wash some of our dirty clothes with the stream so near and the weather so hot and dry."

"You get them out, and I'll wash them," Suzannah offered. "You need your rest. Meanwhile, I'll hang the clothesline between those two tall pine trees over there."

Aunt Ruthie and Aunt Pearl had the same idea, and, before long, the three of them were washing clothes in the stream, though leaning over the boulders to reach the cold water turned out to be backbreaking work.

"If we could only move these boulders out of the way—" Suzannah thought aloud.

No sooner were the words out of her mouth than she remembered what one of the miners had said: "In places where the rivers and streams have washed the gold along, ya might find some gold under the rocks and tree roots."

Maybe there was gold under these very boulders! Her aunts were so busy talking that they weren't paying attention to Suzannah's idle chatter. But now was no time to look. Better to wait until she was alone—

"Why, Suzannah . . . you're going to wear some more holes in your red calico dress, scrubbing so hard," Aunt Ruthie said.

Suzannah sat back on her heels and lifted the garment to take a closer look. "It's mighty dirty."

"Isn't everything?" Aunt Pearl sighed. "I don't see how we'll ever live decently again unless the men do find gold."

"Or the women," Suzannah let slip. She ignored Aunt Ruthie's peculiar look.

As she soaped down a pair of Jamie's blue jumpers, Suzannah examined the stream for tell-tale sparkles of gold, but there was no sign of any. Maybe most of the gold had washed out to the river years ago . . . unless the boulders had trapped some.

"I really like washing clothes," she told her aunts, wondering how she could find time when they weren't with her to look for gold.

Aunt Ruthie blinked. "That's something new! You've never cared much for this chore before."

"But this is such a beautiful place," Suzannah explained. "Just listen to the sound of the stream bubbling along over the rocks and the birds singing. After the desert and the trail and the snowstorm, it's like Paradise!"

"I suppose it is at that," Aunt Pearl agreed. "Pauline ought to sketch some pictures so we can remember this place when we move on."

No sooner had they begun hanging the wet clothes on the clothesline than a rider on a chestnut horse galloped into their camp.

"Hello, ladies," the man called out, doffing his hat with a flourish. "I see you made it to California."

Suzannah almost dropped Jamie's jumper into the

pine needles and dust. *Charles! Charles Herrington!* Secretly she had been hoping he had moved on, that they wouldn't have to see him again. Now here he was, handsome as ever in his black gambler's suit.

"And where's my beautiful wife?"

"Resting in the wagon with Jamie," Suzannah replied, none too kindly. "They're tired and Pauline . . . well, Pauline needs her rest. Best if you don't wake them up."

"I'll be the judge of that," Charles snapped. "Which wagon?"

Suzannah clamped her lips shut, and finally Aunt Ruthie pointed it out. "The middle one."

Aunt Pearl stood up to face him. "You've some nerve . . . just riding up and expecting a wife's welcome after you've left her and a small child on the other side of the Forty-Mile Desert and the Sierra Nevada Mountains!"

Charles smiled. "I knew you fine people would take good care of them. She'll be happy enough to have me when she sees all the gold dust I've been mining."

Suzannah couldn't believe her ears. "Mining . . . in your gambling tent?"

He gave a haughty laugh. "Any fool can stand up to his knees in water all day long, or pickaxe the ground until his back is broken. It takes a real man to earn his living by his wits!" With that, he wheeled Lucky around and rode over to the covered wagons.

Charles dismounted, tied the reins to a wheel, and then peered in through the front of the open canvas.

Suzannah heard the murmur of his voice, then Pauline's. An instant later, she was in his arms. "Oh, Charles . . . I've missed you so much!"

"And I've missed you."

Suzannah spun away, determined not to hear another word from Charles's lying lips!

# CHAPTER
# SEVEN

When Uncle Franklin and Uncle Karl rode up, they were carrying a huge sack of flour and another of potatoes, carrots, and onions.

"There are no stores, no restaurants . . . nothing but thousands of unwashed miners," Uncle Franklin explained. "We bought the last of the supplies a farmer was taking to the tent town down the way, and we paid a fortune for it!"

"A fortune for vegetables?" Aunt Ruthie was dumbfounded.

Uncle Franklin dismounted and began unloading. "You wouldn't believe it. There's more gold than food hereabouts!"

"We got to find some gold," Uncle Karl said, "or we'll be in trouble. On our way back, we saw a likely place to try fer it. Either the miners gave up on it, or they ain't tried it out yet. Wasn't any sign of diggin'."

Suzannah was worried. What if they thought of looking under the boulders in the stream?

"Charles is here," Aunt Ruthie told the men. "He said you told him where to find us."

"Indeed, we did," Uncle Franklin replied. "I also reminded him of his duty to his wife and child.'"

"Shhh. Charles will hear—"

"It won't hurt for him to be reminded."

Just then, Charles climbed out of the wagon with Pauline and Jamie. Either he hadn't heard the conversation about him or was pretending not to, for he seemed more cheerful than usual. "Sounds like more gold miners have arrived to pluck the hills clean."

"Better than fleecin' 'em in your gambling tent," Uncle Karl muttered.

"Karl, dear—" Aunt Pearl gave him a warning look.

But Uncle Franklin thoughtfully changed the subject. "I see that you found our camp easily, Charles."

"My tent is only a mile or so away, and you gave good directions. Now what shall I do with the fine ham I brought along for supper?" he asked, motioning toward the package wrapped in burlap and tied to his saddle bags.

Aunt Ruthie brightened. "How very nice of you, Charles. We haven't had a good ham since we left Missouri."

Charles smiled. "My pleasure. Daniel, be a good lad and get it for us."

Daniel nodded and headed for the chestnut stallion, but Suzannah could see he didn't appreciate being called "a good lad," especially not by Charles Herrington. Ham or not, she was suspicious of Charles, too.

"I'm eager to find some of that gold," Uncle Karl

said. "You men want to come along with us while the women cook supper? Time's a'wastin'!"

"Can I go along?" Suzannah asked.

"Why, Suzannah!" Aunt Ruthie said. "The gold fields are no place for a girl!"

Uncle Franklin nodded his agreement. "I can't blame you for wanting to go, but I don't believe it's a good idea. Not with all those rough miners."

"Should have known you wouldn't let me go," she complained.

Minutes later, Uncle Franklin, Daniel, and Garth rode off with Uncle Karl. "We'll be back in time for supper," Uncle Franklin called back to them.

Suzannah sincerely hoped they wouldn't look under the boulders by the stream. She had a strong feeling about finding gold there and was relieved to see them ride across the stream without stopping.

"May I help start supper?" Pauline asked.

"Why don't you and Jamie visit with Charles instead?" Aunt Ruthie suggested. "You might want to take a walk back along the trail. I'm sure I saw blackberry bushes growing there. It'd be fine to have berries for dessert."

"Thank you, Aunt Ruthie! We'd enjoy that!" Pauline beamed, her flushed face revealing her pleasure in having her husband back. "And Jamie's never been berry picking."

"I'll *walk* along with you," Charles said, his tone of voice making it clear that berry picking was not for him.

*Hmmph!* Suzannah thought. Who did Charles Herrington think he was? He and his fine suit and being too good to bend over and pick a few blackberries!

Before anyone else could think of it, Suzannah grabbed two buckets and headed for the stream. "I'll get the cooking water."

When she reached the stream, Pauline, Charles, and

Jamie were well down the road, their backs to her. And her aunts were getting the cookpots out of the wagons. Now was her chance! She struggled to dislodge a big rock on the edge of the stream.

Just then Aunt Pearl called out, "We need some firewood, Suzannah! Could you find some, please?"

"In a minute!" Suzannah dropped the rock.

*Tarnation!* she thought. Hadn't been any gold under it anyhow. She busied herself filling the water buckets, then hurried back to find wood for the cookfire.

While the women peeled potatoes and chopped the carrots and onions, Suzannah waited for another chance to go to the stream without calling attention to herself.

"With clothes flapping on the line, it's beginning to seem like home here," Aunt Ruthie remarked about their rustic camp. "Or maybe it's because we're planning to stay a while."

Suzannah looked around. The three covered wagons under the cedar trees . . . oxen in the corral . . . pup tents set up for Daniel and Garth to sleep in . . . cookfire flaming beneath the water kettle—

"This is sure better than the wagon trail through the desert and mountains," she admitted, "but it's nothing like a real home."

Aunt Pearl nodded in agreement. "It'll do for a while, but I hope we end up with something as nice as my log house in Missouri. It seems to me that our lives have been going downhill, just like the last lap of our journey through the mountains."

"Now, Pearl, it isn't like you to be discouraged. Besides, maybe the men will find gold soon and we can move on to a more permanent place," Aunt Ruthie said.

Suzannah was tempted to tell them about her strong feeling that there was gold in the stream, then remembered the miner's warning. Instead, she said, "Just look at Lad and Lass rolling in the grass. I do think *they* feel at home."

The aroma of cooking potatoes, carrots, and onions filled the mountain air when the rest of the family returned.

"No blackberries," Pauline said, "but it was a fine outing."

"No gold yet, either," said Uncle Franklin.

"Not one ounce, not one sliver!" Daniel told them. "We did see a miner pry out a bit with his knife, though— gold like fish scales—but it didn't add up to much."

"We were waiting for you to bring back buckets of it," Suzannah joked.

Uncle Franklin gave them a woeful smile. "The strikes aren't as good as they were in the spring. We hear that most of the surface gold is already gone. No one is finding great nuggets just lying about now."

"Maybe we're too late," Aunt Pearl fretted.

"It takes luck," Charles told them. "Some men find a nugget under the very first rock they turn over."

Suzannah clamped her mouth shut. She fervently hoped they wouldn't think to look in the stream. She was already beginning to feel like it belonged to her.

"Some find it in their first pan of water, and others dig halfway to China and barely get enough to keep themselves alive," Charles continued. "But, as I said, it's mostly luck."

"I don't believe in luck," Aunt Ruthie protested. "I believe in God working in people's lives—"

Suzannah scarcely heard what Aunt Ruthie had to say about God, she was so worried about them looking in *her* stream.

"Did you try for gold?" Uncle Karl asked Charles.

"Who, me?"

"Meanin' you'd do better at gamblin'?"

Charles shrugged. "I take my chances—"

"Card-sharkin'!" Uncle Karl said. "Cheatin' folks and fillin' 'em up with hard drink so they can't think straight!"

Aunt Pearl put a hand on his arm. "Karl, dear, let's not have trouble. Charles is Pauline's husband—"

Karl shot his wife an angry look. Turning, he headed for their wagon. Probably he'd sit behind it and carve wood or whittle until he cooled down, Suzannah thought.

"I'm not sure my back will hold up long to digging or panning for gold," said Uncle Franklin. "But if I can get enough money together, I'd like to go down to the valley and bring in wagons of fruit and vegetables for those miners. Their health—and ours—will be ruined without some good food."

Aunt Ruthie gave him a fond look. "I'm glad you're thinking of their health, too, not just our own."

Uncle Franklin shook his head. "I can't imagine why someone hasn't thought of it before now . . . and with doctors here digging for gold themselves! You'd think they'd know better. And it's not just food that's in short supply. There aren't even enough shovels or picks or pans or buckets—the tools every miner needs."

"As soon as I have decent living quarters, I'm hoping Pauline will go back with me to the tent city," Charles remarked. "The miners will pay a lot to have a beautiful lady serve them their drinks."

Suzannah's mouth dropped open. Couldn't he see that Pauline was going to have a baby?

But Aunt Ruthie spoke up boldly. "Surely you don't mean that she is to serve the miners, Charles! Not in her condition!"

"Of course I mean it. She needs to be with her husband, and I need my wife."

Uncle Franklin gave Charles a hard look. "This is no

time for Pauline to be on her feet day and night, waiting on miners. I hope you'll think better of it."

"Well, perhaps later then," Charles said, backing down a little. "Perhaps in a few months. She's probably better off sleeping in the wagon here for now."

Uncle Franklin drew a deep breath. "Let's wash up for supper."

Suzannah swallowed hard as they headed for the stream. What if they turned the rocks over and found her gold? It was her only chance to find some, since they wouldn't let her mine with the men. She watched as Uncle Karl joined the others at the stream. They were washing their hands and faces right by the rocks.

"I'd better wash up, too!" she called out to Aunt Ruthie and raced to the stream. "Please watch the biscuits!"

Fortunately the men had finished and were starting back, and she made fast work of washing her hands for the second time.

Daniel waited for her. "Doesn't that fried ham smell good?"

"Sure does. Even if Charles did bring it." She wiped her wet hands on her old blue gingham dress.

Daniel stared at her. "What's wrong with you today?"

Suzannah shrugged. "Nothing more than usual."

Daniel grinned. As they started back toward the covered wagons, he tugged one of her pigtails.

"Hey! Stop that, Daniel Meriwether Colton!" She twisted away and, laughing, raced him to the cookfire. *Whew! No one had looked under the rocks by the stream yet!*

As they ate their supper on folding stools and in the dried grass, Uncle Franklin was still planning. "The more

I think of it, the more I believe Daniel and I should ride down to the valley, buy a farm wagon and provisions, and bring them back to sell to the miners."

"Why take up grocerin' when there's gold to be found all around?" Uncle Karl wanted to know.

"But what good is gold if people have nothing to eat? In any event, I'm going to have to find gold before going down to the valley to buy food. We're short of funds."

"The thing to bring back is barrels of hard drink," Charles said. "That's where you can make the *real* money. In fact, I'll give you enough money now, with a good profit besides, to buy some for my tent."

Suzannah almost choked on a mouthful of ham. Surely Charles wouldn't expect Uncle Franklin to do such a thing. Or would he?

"Thank you all the same, Charles," Uncle Franklin replied quietly, "but I can't find it in my conscience to buy and sell liquor."

Charles lifted an arched brow. "There aren't too many ways to make a living in the gold fields, you know. Besides searching for gold, there's only doctoring and gambling—"

"We women could take in laundry and wash it here by the stream," Aunt Ruthie suggested.

Uncle Franklin gazed at her tenderly. "Ruthie Colton, I couldn't bear to see you breaking your back, doing laundry for others. It's bad enough that you do it for us."

She patted her husband's hand fondly and smiled up at him.

All through supper, groups of miners walked or rode by on their way home from the gold fields. One passing miner called out, "Smells mighty fine!" Another added, "Ye got grub fer the five of us? We'd pay in gold."

Aunt Ruthie looked at Uncle Franklin. "What do you think?"

"How much food is left?"

She thought for a moment. "Enough for five more, with enough left over for tomorrow."

Uncle Franklin rose to his feet. "How much would each of you pay for one plateful? There's ham, carrots, potatoes with onions, and the best biscuits west of the Continental Divide!"

When the miners named the amount in gold dust, Uncle Franklin's eyes widened. He turned to Aunt Ruthie, Aunt Pearl, and Uncle Karl. "What do you think?"

They nodded their approval.

"It'd be a beginnin'," Uncle Karl said. "The first income our family's had since we left Missouri. I'll tie up the dogs so they aren't snappin' at 'em."

"Well, then," Uncle Franklin said to the miners, "you can wash up at the stream and come for supper."

*Wash up at the stream!* Suzannah was horrified.

Aunt Ruthie and Aunt Pearl jumped to their feet and headed for the cookfire, with Suzannah and Pauline close behind. "We'll have to make more biscuits . . . add a bit of water to the vegetables—"

Suzannah worked as fast as she could, all the while keeping an eye on the miners to see if they were looking under the boulders by the stream. She guessed they didn't, since there were millions of other places to look, and they were too hungry to think about gold right now anyhow.

Finally, the miners dried their hands on their pants and joined the circle around the cookfire.

While Uncle Franklin and Uncle Karl offered stools to the miners, Suzannah helped the women dish up the food.

"We've got a broken folding table we brought on the journey west," said Uncle Franklin. "We could fix it up."

"Sounds fine. We're used to settin' on the ground," said the red-headed leader of the miners, then introduced himself. "I'm Octavius Brooks, but I go by the name of Big Red."

Suzannah saw the reason why. He was tall and broad-shouldered, and his hair was dark red and as wavy as his fine beard. What held her attention, though, was the warm glow in his brown eyes.

Big Red introduced the others: "Eli Pringle, John Thompson, Stuart Huckinger, and Oliver Durston. We been out here in the diggin's since spring."

As the miners settled down, Charles ambled over to his horse. He looked over the miners, then called back to Pauline, "We'll soon see what's beneath your family's fine dignity."

The next morning, the same five miners were back for breakfast, bringing two of their friends. "Got anythin' to eat?" called Big Red.

"Potato flapjacks and ham," replied Aunt Ruthie, wiping her floury hands on her apron.

"Sounds good, ma'am," he said. "Jest in case, we brought our own coffee."

Suzannah wasn't so sure they should feed them since their own men had already headed for the gold fields. On the other hand, Lad and Lass stood guard. "How much will you pay?" she asked.

"Why, Suzannah!" Aunt Ruthie exclaimed.

"It's no matter, Miz Colton." Big Red smiled, showing a fine set of white teeth. "Hereabouts it don't hurt to find out first if folks can pay."

When the men decided the amount they'd pay in gold dust, Aunt Ruthie glanced toward Aunt Pearl.

"Fine," Aunt Pearl agreed. "Come along, then. Have a seat at the table, and I'll put on the coffee."

Suzannah got out the tin plates and cups, and set the rickety table. "We don't have napkins," she told them. "Not that we've had any since we left Aunt Pearl's cabin in Missouri."

They burst out laughing. "Ought to call it the 'No Napkin Restaurant'," Big Red said.

Suzannah managed a short laugh herself. "We don't have much of anything else, for that matter. We're just glad to have enough food for the day. Maybe we ought to call it the 'High Hopes Restaurant'."

"High Hopes . . . jest like most of us miners. That's a right good name."

When they finished breakfast, Eli Pringle gave some welcome news. "There's a farmer down the road at that tent town today, with beef cattle and other things fer sale. Maybe ye could get provisions from him."

As soon as the miners left, Aunt Pearl was quick to follow up on the miner's suggestion. "Suzannah and I could hitch up the oxen to my wagon and go down to see about buying provisions."

"You could try," Aunt Ruthie said. "But we don't have much gold yet. Best if I stay here with Pauline and Jamie."

Aunt Pearl shrugged. "We'll leave Lad and Lass with you. If our men don't find gold, we'll have to use our wits."

Suzannah wondered if she'd ever have a chance to look under the boulders. Not this morning. She'd have to yoke the oxen and hitch them to the wagon.

Before long, she and Aunt Pearl were on the way down the road in her aunt's covered wagon. As they neared the tent town, they could see more and more miners panning gold in the streams and digging in trenches. When she and Aunt Pearl passed, the men stopped their work to stare at them.

"Pretend not to notice," Aunt Pearl said. "Just pretend we're walking to town at home."

Suzannah couldn't help laughing. "People would stare in Alexandria, Virginia, too, if they saw two women driving oxen and a covered wagon down the street!"

Aunt Pearl had to smile. "Now they would at that, wouldn't they?"

Just then they passed by a dingy white tent with a badly painted sign spelling out: THE HERRINGTON PALACE.

"So that's Charles's gambling tent," said Aunt Pearl. "Good thing he changed his mind about expecting Pauline and Jamie to live here in this filth."

Finally they found the farmer with his wagon full of provisions, and a fine herd of beef cattle tied on behind. Miners were lined up by the tailgate, and it took only a few minutes to see they were paying high prices for everything.

"I'll give ye a dollar's worth of gold dust fer yer last egg," one of them offered the farmer.

"A dollar for an egg!" Suzannah exclaimed to her aunt. "I've never heard of such high prices!"

"If we're going to run a restaurant, we'll need eggs and vegetables," said Aunt Pearl, a worried look on her face. "And one of those beef cattle, too."

Suzannah looked the cattle over. "I guess I could drive one back to our camp, but how would we ever pay for it?"

"I think this is a time for prayer," said her aunt.

Suzannah closed her eyes and set right to it.

When they arrived at the front of the line, Aunt Pearl bought sacks of carrots, onions, potatoes, apples, and a piece of beef for dinner. "I'd like one of your beef cattle, too," she said to the farmer, "but we don't have enough money with us. I could pay you tomorrow."

"Cain't let you have it on credit," he said. "Lots o' work, drivin' them cattle up here to the foothills."

Aunt Pearl nodded. "I'm sure it is. And it's lots of work starting a restaurant, too. We need meat for our customers."

Just then Big Red stepped up. "I'll buy that beef for these ladies," he told the farmer, getting out his gold pouch. When Aunt Pearl began to protest, he told her, "You can pay me off in meals . . . and the rest in gold when you get some."

"You're an answer to prayer!" Aunt Pearl said.

Big Red gave them a fine white smile. "I'm a prayin' man myself. I'll be at your place tonight for supper, and I'll bring you some more payin' customers."

On the way back to the camp, Aunt Pearl was overjoyed. "I can scarcely believe it. We prayed for a way to get that beef, and Big Red was right there to buy it for us! Wait till I tell Ruthie! Isn't God good?"

"He is!" Suzannah agreed. But as she drove the beef cow along the dusty trail, she felt a sudden wave of homesickness. What she wouldn't give to be in Alexandria this morning, sitting in the schoolroom with her best friend, Jenny, instead of driving a beef cow through the gold fields of California!

At suppertime, the mingled aromas of beef stew and apple cobbler wafted through the air. As promised, Big Red was there with ten other miners.

"I've been tellin' the men about your good cookin'," he said. "Half of 'em haven't had anything decent to eat in months, and them who saw you come in for provisions already know about the High Hopes Restaurant."

"*I'm* hopin' you made plenty stew!" one of them said.

"We sure did," Suzannah replied. "My sister and I have never peeled so many potatoes or cut up so many carrots and onions in our lives!"

Uncle Karl shook his head in disbelief. "By golly, these women are better at gettin' gold than we are. We'd better build another table and make some benches."

"And butcher the beef cow tomorrow morning?" Aunt Pearl asked.

Uncle Karl gave a nod of consent.

"And put up a sign by the road?" Aunt Ruthie added. "The High Hopes Restaurant . . . maybe Pauline can give it her artistic touch."

Uncle Franklin laughed. "At the rate things are going, you won't need a sign. Just the smell of your beef stew and apple cobbler is bringing in customers. Look, here come more now."

"Ye open to the public?" one of them asked.

"Appears like it," said Uncle Franklin. "It appears that we've got ourselves an outdoor restaurant."

That evening as the miners ate supper, the men from the cabins across the road brought out a fiddle and an accordion, and sat on their doorstoops. Before long, the air was filled with the melodies of "Old Dan Tucker," "The Last Rose of Summer," and "Do They Miss Me at Home?" Uncle Franklin took out his harmonica and played along.

It seemed that the miners, who had worked hard all day in the hot sun, loved nothing better than to set aside their day's work in the evening and sing or make music. The ravines and gulches vibrated with it.

"Ever heard the Boston Boy play his bugle?" one of the men asked Suzannah.

"No," she replied, removing the dirty tin plates from the table.

"Keep listenin'. Maybe he'll play tonight."

At bedtime, she heard the bugler. The strains of "Oft in the Stilly Night" and "The Red, White, and Blue" echoed through the darkness. As she lay down in the covered wagon with Pauline and Jamie, "The Star Spangled Banner" rang out in the night, reminding her that no matter how far they had come from Virginia, they were still in America.

Plumping the pillow beneath her head, Suzannah thought of the day's activities. Who would have ever thought they'd be starting a business on the banks of a stream in California? And, speaking of streams, what would happen if any of those miners who were coming to eat with them ever decided to check out "her" stream for gold?

She almost felt she had staked her claim there. All she needed was a big sign, saying, "NO TRESPASSING! THIS MEANS YOU!"

# CHAPTER
# EIGHT

O<sub>h</sub> ...!"

Pauline's whisper in the early dawn hours awakened Suzannah out of a deep sleep. And just in time, too. In her dreams, she was fighting off a horde of angry miners who had invaded her stream with pans and pickaxes.

When Suzannah looked over at Pauline, her sister's eyes were wide. "What's wrong? Are you sick?"

Pauline shook her head. "It's just that the baby is kicking so hard. Do you ... do you want to feel it?"

Suzannah was curious. She had never felt an unborn baby kick. She reached out her hand from under the quilt and let Pauline guide it to her rounded stomach.

At first she didn't feel anything. Then there was a faint flutter. "Doesn't that hurt?"

Pauline smiled. "Not a bit. I guess God made our

bodies to take a lot. The Bible says we are 'fearfully and wonderfully made.'"

Suzannah thought about that. It all seemed like such a miracle that right this minute a new little person was moving and kicking inside her sister's body, just waiting until he or she was big enough and strong enough to be born.

Suddenly embarrassed, Suzannah pulled her hand back under the covers. People didn't talk about having babies, and she didn't know any girls back in Virginia who'd ever felt an unborn baby kick.

"If it's a girl," Pauline said, "I'm going to name her Anna Ruth. Anna for you since we can't have two Suzannahs in one family, and Ruth for Aunt Ruthie."

Suzannah stared, awestruck. "I never thought I'd have a baby named for *me*."

"Well, you will . . . if it's a girl. I thought we could call her Annie while she's little."

"What if it's a boy?"

Pauline said, "I'm thinking of Octavius, like Big Red."

"Octavius? Oh, Pauline, you're joking!"

Pauline muffled a laugh with her hand. "I am. If it's a boy, I've been thinking of Danford Franklin for Daniel and Uncle Franklin."

"What does Charles say about that?"

Pauline pushed back her golden hair. "He doesn't care. He says naming a baby is the mother's job."

Feeling that her sister might be getting upset, Suzannah quickly said, "Well, just don't middle-name it 'Meriwether,' or it might have itchy feet like Uncle Franklin and Daniel!" Both her uncle and cousin had been named for the great explorer, Captain Meriwether Lewis.

"I promise," Pauline said, smiling once again. "No Meriwether and no Octavius."

Suzannah dared to ask, "When do you think it will
. . . happen?"

"Soon," Pauline said with a smile. "Soon."

Suzannah wondered if they'd still be living in the
wagon when the baby was born. On the journey west,
many a baby had been born in a covered wagon, but it
seemed to her that a warm house would be better.

Later, when she climbed out of the wagon, she looked
across the road at the five cabins in the distance. According
to Big Red, the cabins had been built in '44 by settlers who
had sold them to miners before they moved on. Though the
shanties were small and plain, they would be a sight better
for a newborn baby than a covered wagon!

When she saw Uncle Franklin, Suzannah was burst-
ing with her new idea. "Do you think we could build some
cabins like those across the road?"

He looked about at the tall hardwood trees. "Easy
enough, I'd think," he said. "But with winter coming on,
we won't be staying long enough to need them. Soon there
will be no sure way of making a living."

"The restaurant and gold digging—"

He shook his head. "In a few weeks these foothills will
be covered with snow. Some of the miners are already
moving on down to the valley or into San Francisco. Most
say they're coming back in the spring in hopes that the
rains will wash down more gold."

"Then what will we do?"

"We haven't decided yet. But I'm in favor of moving
just outside the city. I fear this gold rush is bringing in
more and more men who'd rather steal gold than dig or
pan for it themselves. These gold fields will be no place for
women and children."

"But Pauline and her baby—" Suzannah paused,
blushing.

Uncle Franklin smiled kindly. "We won't travel for a

while yet. In the meantime, it seems wisest to continue what we're doing—looking for gold and running the restaurant. Unfortunately, the farmers have stopped bringing up supplies from the valley. So today Daniel, Big Red, and I are going down to buy food and some cold weather supplies for the miners who are staying the winter—boots, flannel shirts, coats, blankets, and such."

"If there's nothing to do, why would they stay through the winter?"

"Gold fever," he replied. "They can't stay away from it any more than Charles can stay away from his gambling, or other men from hard drink."

*Gold fever.* She spent most of her waking hours waiting for a chance to be alone so she could look for gold under the boulders in the stream. And at night, her dreams were filled with visions of gold, or of people trying to take it away from her. If that was gold fever, she was afraid she had it.

At breakfast, they fed twenty miners. As soon as Uncle Franklin drained his coffee cup, he and Daniel and Big Red mounted their horses and started down to the valley to buy provisions.

"Take care of yourselves," Uncle Franklin called back. "We'll be back as soon as we can."

Uncle Karl and Garth got their gold pans and pickaxes together. "Maybe today we'll strike it rich," said her uncle.

To Suzannah's great surprise, Garth smiled at his stepmother. "I'll string all of my nuggets into a gold necklace for you."

Aunt Pearl slipped an arm around his shoulders and gave him a hug. "It would be the finest present anyone ever gave me!"

Garth's face turned a little red, and he pulled away, but he didn't try to hide his pleasure.

Suzannah couldn't help thinking how much Garth had changed recently. He had been the meanest, the rudest boy she'd ever known! Even knowing *why* hadn't helped much, though she felt sorry about his mother being killed by Indians. Still, he'd been full of hatred for everyone, not just the Indians. That is, until the day Daniel had stopped him from shooting the Indian girl back on the trail—

"Gold nugget necklace or not, you fellows be sure to be back at midday for dinner," Aunt Pearl said.

When the miners finished their breakfast and pushed back from the table, one of them had an idea. "There's blackberries on the bushes over near the next gulch. Just watch out for bears. They're headin' up to the foothills."

"Blackberry pie would taste mighty good for dinner, wouldn't it?" said Aunt Ruthie.

"Our menfolks would be pleased," Aunt Pearl agreed. "I can carry Karl's rifle in case we see a grizzly. I know how to use it. Had to shoot a wolf once back in Missouri."

"Then I'll stay here and clear up the dishes," Suzannah offered. "Besides, someone needs to stay with Pauline and Jamie."

Aunt Ruthie smiled at her. "That's thoughtful of you, Suzannah." Looking at her sister, she cocked her head and put her hands on her hips. "Then what do you say, Pearl? Shall we go berry picking together like we used to when we were girls?"

Suzannah's hopes rose. With only Pauline and Jamie about, she might have a chance to search along the stream for gold. Pauline tired more easily than ever now. Maybe she could talk her sister into taking a long nap with Jamie later.

Aunt Ruthie and Aunt Pearl took the buckets and made their way down the road. Despite the rifle Aunt Pearl carried, they were giggling as they left the camp.

"You'd think they were girls again," said Pauline, smiling.

"I wouldn't be surprised to hear them break into an old berrying song," Suzannah said.

"Or see those neat blond knots of hair on the back of their heads turn into pigtails," Pauline added.

After their aunts disappeared around the hillside, Pauline offered to dry the dishes. "If I sit on a stool, I can manage."

Suzannah rolled up the sleeves of her red calico dress. It would take a while to wash all of the dishes, pots, and pans. But after that, she'd think of some way to get rid of Pauline so she could hunt gold.

"What are you thinking about so seriously?" Pauline asked.

Suzannah shrugged, not wanting to give away her plan.

Once they'd finished the dishes, she said, "Daniel found a board for our restaurant sign. Could you sketch the letters for him to carve in?"

"Nothing I'd like better!" Pauline said. "I've been feeling so useless lately. Let's find a bit of wood for Jamie so he can make a sign, too."

Jamie looked up at them, laughing, and Pauline ruffled his curls, bleached nearly as blond as her own from the sun.

Bright rays of sunshine filtered through the trees, but Suzannah chose the shadiest spot for Pauline to do her sign-sketching. And she made sure that Pauline's back was to the stream as she settled on a stool.

"Too bad I don't have a ruler to measure out the letters," Pauline said.

"It doesn't matter if you mark it wrong the first time. You've got all the time in the world," Suzannah told her. "While you're working, I thought I'd go down to the stream and look for greens for dinner," she went on carefully, so as not to arouse suspicion. "You know how Aunt Pearl is about greens. She's so afraid we're all going to get scurvy!"

Pauline was already absorbed in her sketch, so Suzannah grabbed a burlap sack and a bucket and started for the stream. Hurrying over the rocks and dried grasses, she looked all around. There were huge boulders surrounding the corral, and other boulders scattered here and there. How would she ever be able to turn the big ones over?

At the stream, she splashed a bucket in the water for Pauline's benefit, then began to push aside a boulder. No gold. The next boulder was even larger, but she heaved and tugged until she moved it just enough to feel around under it. No gold there, either.

From her spot under the trees, Pauline called out, "What are you doing, Suzannah?"

Suzannah pried up another boulder. "I thought there might be greens growing under these rocks."

"Mind you don't find snakes instead!" Pauline warned.

Suzannah gave a little shiver. She looked all around, but didn't see any.

"Or black widow spiders," Pauline added. "Or bears!"

"I'm not worried!" Suzannah yelled. She tipped up another boulder. Nothing.

After Pauline finished her work on the sign, she wandered over to the stream with Jamie, and Suzannah quickly tossed some dandelion greens in the bucket. "That ought to be enough," she said, trying not to sound disappointed.

They strolled back toward the wagons. "You're looking awfully tired, Pauline," Suzannah said. "Why don't you and Jamie take a nap now while it's quiet?"

"I *am* tired," Pauline admitted, putting a hand to her back. "My back aches all the time now. Maybe I'll just lie down for a little while with Jamie."

Once they were settled in the wagon, Suzannah headed for the stream's quiet backwater near the corral. She pulled aside some algae-covered rocks. No sign of any gold here.

When one of the oxen wandered over to visit, she reached up and scratched him behind the ears, stopping to think what to do next. Maybe there wasn't any gold at all in this stream. Maybe there had never been any, or it had been discovered long ago. She was probably just wasting her time.

Still, something drove her on. Spotting a sturdy stick, she picked it up and began to dig in the mud around the rocks. She poked here and there, but felt nothing unusual. Then, probing deeper, the stick hit something solid. She laid the stick aside, knelt down, and began to dig with her hands, pulling up a small rock.

She stared at the muddy object. It didn't look very promising. Swishing it through the water, Suzannah washed away the mud. Then, with the rock in the palm of her hand, she held it up to the light. A stray sunbeam piercing the overhanging branches touched the stone, dazzling her with its glitter. Gold! Real gold! Not as big as the walnut-sized nugget the miner had shown them. More the size of an acorn. But it felt reassuringly heavy.

She threw it into her sack and dug again. Another nugget . . . then another and another! She glanced over to see if anyone was watching, but Pauline and Jamie were still asleep. She dug frantically now. A whole pocket of nuggets. Twelve more! She washed them and tossed them into the sack.

Pulling aside another rock, she found three more nuggets with no effort at all. Upending one rock after another, she collected nuggets until the bottom of the burlap sack was full.

She remembered what the miner had said about not telling anyone, not even your best friend. Since Jenny was still in Virginia, she guessed that meant Daniel. It would be hard not to let her cousin in on her discovery, but it was a secret she meant to keep.

She was still finding nuggets when Aunt Ruthie and Aunt Pearl returned from berrying.

"Whatever are you doing back there?" Aunt Ruthie asked.

"Just foolin' around," she told them innocently.

"Sure you're not looking for gold?" Aunt Pearl

chimed in. "I heard one of the miners say this morning that we ought to try this stream. I think I'll just do that after dinner, when everyone has left. Wouldn't the men be surprised if we were the ones who found gold right under our very noses?"

"What would you do with it?" asked Aunt Ruthie.

Aunt Pearl thought for a moment. "Since Karl wants to stay here, I'd see about buying those cabins across the road so we could at least be warm this winter."

Suzannah drew a deep breath, glad she'd found the gold first. She'd have to hide it in the bottom of her trunk later. She was pretty sure she'd gotten most of it out, maybe all of it. On the other hand, she couldn't help feeling a little guilty about not sharing it, too.

Overhead, flocks of birds flew south, but the fine weather held. Now, though, there wasn't enough water for the miners to wash out the gold. The streams dried up, and even the one out front was down to a trickle.

Garth and Uncle Karl prospected the stream out front and even the quiet backwater by the corral, but they found no more gold. And when they returned to the other diggings, they came back to camp with just enough gold to help buy food.

In spite of the disappointment, Uncle Karl was determined. "We ain't about to give up."

Suzannah was tempted to tell him about the layer of gold nuggets lining the bottom of her trunk. Instead, she said, "Well, the restaurant is doing fine. We're earning more gold than most of the miners and staying well-fed ourselves!"

Garth nodded. "Every miner around Coloma knows of the High Hopes Restaurant. But they'll leave when the heavy rains and snow come. Pa figgers we've got to find gold to make it through the winter, then come out again next spring."

Suzannah bit her lips shut.

Early Friday afternoon, Big Red returned with a wagon pulled by mules. Behind it, Daniel drove ten beef cattle.

"Open the corral gate!" he yelled.

Suzannah rushed to the gate. "Where's Uncle Franklin?"

"Mother won't like it," he began, "but Father's still in the valley buying a farm wagon and more provisions. He'll come later."

"But where did you get the money?" she wanted to know.

"Cattle are cheap down in the valley," Daniel said, "and Big Red lent us money for the rest."

Suzannah felt another pang of guilt. She could have helped buy those provisions with the gold she'd found. And she could certainly repay Big Red. But if she told them about it, they might say the gold belonged to all of them and she'd never see it again. Besides, she needed it to help take care of Pauline and Jamie.

"Big Red's a fine friend," Daniel said. "He showed us where to buy produce and cattle and even yellow flannel for . . . for Pauline to make little blankets." He rushed on, his face red. "He's only been here since spring, but everybody knows and likes him. Just look at him now!"

Suzannah turned to see what Daniel was talking about. Big Red was tossing Jamie into the air, then tickling him with his red beard. The little boy giggled with delight. Beside them, Pauline looked on with pleasure. Big Red wasn't handsome like Charles, but he sure was a fine fellow.

As Suzannah watched Big Red and Jamie, an idea

struck. But she waited until the others were busy putting away provisions and driving the beef cattle into the corral to put her idea into action.

Big Red was still playing with Jamie when she approached him with her plan. "How much would it cost to buy one of those cabins across the road?"

Setting Jamie on his shoulders, Big Red looked her in the eye, probably wondering why a young girl would want to know. "No idea. But I'd be glad to find out. In fact, I can amble over there right now. Wouldn't hurt to take Jamie with me so I don't look quite so . . . imposing."

He called to Pauline as she helped the aunts store the provisions. "Can I borrow Jamie a spell? I need to talk to those miners across the road for a few minutes."

"Yes, of course," Pauline said. "Not too long, though. He needs his afternoon nap."

Big Red turned to Suzannah. "It might take a goodly amount of gold to buy a cabin. Maybe you folks could rent for a while."

"Uncle Franklin wants to move on to San Francisco this winter. We'd only need it for . . . a few more weeks." *Until Pauline has the baby,* she meant, and had a feeling he knew exactly what she was thinking. "How much is a nugget worth . . . a nugget about the size of an acorn?"

He raised his eyebrows. "Maybe more than before, now that most of the miners are leavin'."

Suzannah watched as he bounced Jamie merrily along on their way to the road, then as he approached the cabins. There was usually a miner or two around, digging in the back of the property.

*Maybe I should pray about this,* she thought, almost skipping with excitement. But she figured Big Red had prayed enough already to cover them both.

# CHAPTER
# NINE

Good news," Big Red told Suzannah when he returned. "Those miners are goin' back East any day now. Guess they made good strikes. But they want to sell, not rent."

Suzannah swallowed. "Sell? How much do they want?"

Big Red named a large figure, and her heart sank. "That much?"

He nodded. "They say they won't have any trouble sellin' to miners who are plannin' to stay the winter."

"Only someone who's *already* struck it rich could pay that much!" she retorted. "Besides, Uncle Franklin says anyone can build cabins with so many trees about."

"Generally, miners with gold fever won't stop searchin' for gold long enough to build a cabin. They'd just as soon live in a cave or a tent."

She scuffed the toe of her old kid boot in the dust. There it was again: *gold fever*. More and more often, she found herself yearning to be out hunting gold instead of working at the High Hopes Restaurant. And, whenever she had a chance, she still looked for it in the backwater of the stream near their camp. Not that she'd found any more since that first day.

"Maybe I'll buy the cabins myself," Big Red said. "They even have a corral out back for horses. Unless I miss my guess, there'll be miners comin' next year, and I can resell the cabins then. Come on, Jamie, let's go visitin' again."

Suzannah watched him hurry through the trees and jump the stream to the road. Maybe she'd have time to look between the boulders now, she thought. But no. There was Pauline sitting on a bench by the wagon, hemming a yellow flannel baby blanket.

When Big Red returned, he was grinning from ear to ear. "You're lookin' at the new owner of five cabins. I'll live in one myself and rent the others out." He laughed. "Never figgered to be a landlord! Maybe you and yer folks could be my first renters. That is, if you want to. I'd charge a fair price."

Suzannah felt her mouth drop open, and Big Red chuckled. He explained that the cabins were small, with only three or four bunks each.

"The important thing is to get Pauline inside before . . . before the rains start," she said. "I'll rent one cabin for Pauline, Jamie, and me for the first month, but you have to promise not to tell anyone I paid for it."

"You got my word," he said. "Now, those men are movin' out tomorrow mornin'. The cabins will take some cleanin', but your landlord will give you a hand. Here . . . I guess Jamie wants down if I'm not going to jounce him."

Suzannah reached up for Jamie and whirled him

around in a hug. "Jamie, Jamie! Did you hear that? We're
going to have a real roof over our heads!"

When she found Pauline, Suzannah was beside
herself. "Wait till you hear what's happened. We've got
. . . the use of a cabin—"

Pauline's blue eyes widened. "But we can't begin to
pay for it. We don't have any money left."

"I found some gold!" Suzannah clapped a hand over
her mouth. She couldn't believe what she'd done. In her
haste, she'd let out her secret. "Don't tell anyone, Pauline.
Please don't tell."

Just then Big Red arrived, and without further
explanation, she ran to the wagon. Inside, she unlocked
her trunk, then reached down under her clothes for the
burlap sack. She got out a nugget and slipped it into the
pocket of her dress.

Later, she gave it to Big Red. "Will that be enough?"

He nodded. "Enough for a couple of months. You're
due some back. You must have found a good pocket."

"The bottom of a burlap sack full," she bragged, then
clamped her lips shut.

"I keep a secret," he said, "but don't tell no one
else."

"I—I've already told Pauline. But she won't tell."

"Not easy to keep it a secret, is it?"

She shook her head. "And when I promised myself I
wouldn't tell *anyone!*"

The next morning, from across the road, Suzannah
watched the miners move out of the cabins. When the
restaurant closed after the midday meal, she hurried over
with Big Red.

Since all the cabins were alike, Suzannah chose the

middle one, thinking it would be the safest now that Jamie was running around exploring everything.

When Big Red opened the door, the chinked log walls looked warm and welcoming. And the plank shutters to the two windows stood open, giving them a view of the trees.

"Be nice to have window glass someday," he said. "But you'll be fine for a while, at least 'til the rainy weather sets in."

"There's even furniture!" Suzannah was thrilled.

"It's not much."

But Suzannah was just as pleased with the rustic table and benches in the middle of the room and the four wooden cots built against the log walls as if they had been the finest polished wood.

"And look at the rocking chairs made out of flour barrels!" She threw back her head and laughed.

Big Red chuckled. "Reckon the rockers will come in handy for your sister . . . before long."

"Guess so." It wouldn't be proper to discuss the baby with him, even though he'd been the one who'd found the yellow flannel for the baby blankets. Still, she did wish she could talk to someone about it—anyone but Pauline.

Instead, she and Big Red talked about the stone-lined fireplace while he began to build a fire to take off the chill. By the time Pauline arrived with Jamie, the fire was blazing, casting a cheerful glow about the room. Already, the cabin seemed more like a home.

"A wooden floor!" Pauline marveled. "It's all so much nicer than I even dreamed it could be."

After Daniel had driven the oxen and covered wagon into the corral, he stepped into the cabin and looked around. "All you need now are some curtains at the windows, a wool rug on the floor, and window glass, and you'd have a house as grand as the one in Virginia!"

Suzannah poked his shoulder hard. "Daniel Colton!"

It still hurt to remember the large brick house they'd left behind in Alexandria because of Charles's gambling.

He tugged her pigtail, then ducked before she could strike back. "I'll get your things from the wagon," he said.

Pauline sighed. "I do wish I could be of more help."

"Just have a seat in one of our fine rockers and direct the moving," Suzannah told her.

Pauline eyed the larger of the two barrel rockers and frowned. "What if I get stuck in it?"

Big Red chuckled. "Reckon we'd pull you out or take the barrel staves apart from under you. Now you just settle, Miz Herrin'ton, and rock to your heart's content."

"You've been a real friend to us," she said to Big Red.

"My pleasure."

Suzannah was glad Charles wasn't here to hear Pauline and Big Red making friends. Charles wouldn't like it one bit.

Thinking of Charles stirred the old anger she could never quite overcome. She grabbed the homemade broom next to the fireplace and attacked the dirt as if it were Charles himself. First, she swept the cobwebs from the rafters and the log walls, then she went after the dust on the floor.

Before long, Daniel and Big Red brought in the trunks and placed them at the foot of the bunks.

"Do you always keep your trunk locked?" Daniel asked her.

Suzannah thought fast. "Of course I do! You think I want mice and rats getting into my clothes?"

"Guess not," Daniel said.

She shook out the bedding and quilts, then put them on each bunk. Now the place looked halfway civilized, though she'd be glad for a real bed again.

Noticing that Jamie was trying to climb into the other rocker, Suzannah picked up her nephew and settled him into the chair, tilting it back and forth to start the rhythm. Laughing with delight, he began to rock harder and harder until the whole rocking chair was traveling across the uneven plank floor.

"What you really need," said Daniel when the laughter had died down, "is a big bear rug like the one in that French trapper's cabin on the National Road."

Suzannah rolled her eyes.

"Tell us about it," invited Big Red, scooping up Jamie from the rocker and sitting down with him before the cheery fire.

Suzannah and Daniel pulled up a bench. And when they'd finished the story of the lonely French trapper in the woods of Indiana, Big Red shook his head. "May God preserve me from ever becomin' like that. Can you imagine . . . a man with an invisible wife?"

"Oh, that would never happen to you!" Pauline protested. "You like people too much."

Big Red smiled at her. "The Lord gave me His love for folks, that's all." Changing the subject, he added, "Now I'd best fix up a rail for Jamie's bunk so he don't fall out of bed."

When Aunt Ruthie came over later to see the cabin, she was delighted. "Oh, my dears, you'll be so much better off here than in the wagon." She looked around, taking stock. "Maybe . . . maybe we could rent two of the other cabins until we leave. Especially with the rains coming—" She brightened as the idea grew. "We could even move the restaurant here!"

"Don't see why not," said Big Red. "I'd be glad to have you as renters, if I can eat in your restaurant."

"Well–l–l—" Aunt Ruthie began doubtfully. "We don't have much money."

"Then I'll rent it to you on trust. When your husband gets back with a wagon of goods, he'll have profit."

It occurred to Suzannah that she could afford to rent cabins for all of her family with the gold she'd found, but something held her back. Still, she had to do *something*.

"With Pauline and me living here," she began, "we won't be needing our oxen and wagon. Maybe Daniel could take it down to the valley for more supplies . . . to make more profit."

"A good idea," Aunt Ruthie said, and Suzannah felt guiltier than ever. "While we're here," her aunt went on, "I'd like to see the other cabins, though I'll have to speak to Franklin about renting one when he gets back."

Again Big Red proved to be their friend. "I'll hold one for you until then."

At dinnertime, Aunt Ruthie and Aunt Pearl made a fresh pot of beef stew for the High Hopes Restaurant. "Same kind of stew," she told the miners, "but this time with dumplings. I'm sorry we don't have anything else to cook. My husband hasn't come back yet with the rest of the supplies." Suzannah could tell that Aunt Ruthie was beginning to worry about him.

"Well, it sure beats eatin' beans and jerky every meal," said one of the miners.

"Our cookin's so bad that one fellow ate half-cooked rice and almost died when his stomach swelled up!" another miner said. "Anything you cook would be an improvement over that!"

Suzannah knew that Aunt Ruthie wasn't satisfied. She'd been talking about the supplies she needed—apples, chicken for fricassee, pork for chops and roasts.

"If Father hasn't come back by tomorrow," Daniel said, "I'll go for supplies. But we can barely afford onions and potatoes."

Big Red reached for his gold pouch. "I'll lend you some gold dust so you can buy meat and anythin' else you need."

"You must have found a lot of gold," Suzannah guessed.

"I did all right."

She was tempted to tell him about her find, but how could she when Big Red was always lending them gold? Of course, he already knew she had found some, but what would he think of her when he learned she had enough to support her whole family and hadn't told them?

Aunt Ruthie and Aunt Pearl sat down to make up a shopping list. "I just wish you didn't have to go alone, Daniel," said Aunt Pearl as she wrote the list.

"Yes, be careful," Aunt Ruthie warned.

And before Suzannah knew it, they were seeing Daniel off. Suzannah watched her cousin climb up onto the driver's seat, bullwhip in hand. She wished she could go along to help. But she shrugged aside the thought. She had to help Pauline. And besides, she was living only for the next time she could search the stream for more gold!

It wasn't Daniel who was sitting on the driver's seat of her wagon the next evening when it rolled into camp. It was one of the miners who ate at their restaurant. And when she saw Daniel lying unconscious on the floor of the wagon, she shook all over.

"Robbers," the miner told them. "But I didn't see who done it. They rode off before I could git a good look."

"Oh, Daniel—" Suzannah whispered.

Aunt Ruthie's face was white as she felt Daniel's neck for a pulse. "He's alive. Oh, thank God, he's alive! Why didn't I wait for Franklin before I sent Daniel away? I should never have sent him to the valley alone!"

Suzannah hoped they wouldn't remember that it was *her* idea. "Please let him sleep in my bunk," she begged.

After Daniel was settled in, he opened his eyes, but his gaze was vacant, and he didn't say a word.

"I'm speakin' fer the family now," said Uncle Karl, who had returned from his hunting trip with Garth. "We'll rent two more cabins. Garth and I got jest enough gold fer it. I thought the dogs would protect us, but with a roof over our heads, we'll be considerable safer."

The next morning when Daniel awakened in the cabin, he was able to recall some of what had happened. "I was hurrying the oxen along through the last light of day when suddenly . . . wham! . . . something hit me."

"That's all you remember?" Suzannah asked.

He nodded, wincing at the pain in his head.

"We heard of other robberies last night," she went on. "Two farmers' wagons . . . and even Charles's gambling tent."

"I hope Father's safe . . . wherever he is."

Suzannah stared in silence at the India-rubber sheet they had hung over the shutters to keep out the rain. Big drops splatted against the sheet in a steady downpour. With the beginning of the rainy season, only a few miners showed up at the restaurant now. And most of them were heading down from the foothills.

"I guess the miners who didn't find much gold will do anything to get some before they go into San Francisco," she said.

"And now we owe Big Red the gold he's loaned us." Even with a headache, Daniel was thinking clearly.

Again Suzannah's conscience gave her a twinge. Still, the robbery wasn't *her* fault. Best not to think about it too much.

Despite the rain, Uncle Karl and Garth brought the covered wagons and the restaurant tables over from across the road so their families could move into the two other cabins. Inside Suzannah's cabin, the women were sewing together the white canvas covers from two of the wagons to make an awning. They planned to stretch it between the cabins for their new restaurant.

While they worked, Aunt Ruthie worried about her husband. "We must pray for Franklin," she said. "Suzannah, you've always believed in prayer, so keep praying for your uncle."

She tried. She really tried. But lately it seemed her prayers rose no higher than the ceiling of the cabin.

Late the next day, when the rain stopped, the miners found that the High Hopes Restaurant had moved across the road. The new awning hung between the two cabins, forming a droopy roof. But at least it protected the tables from the dripping trees.

As darkness fell, Suzannah brought lighted lanterns to the tables, then set the places for supper. In the flickering light, the restaurant looked very inviting.

Right after supper, Uncle Franklin rolled in with a wagonload of goods and a stranger right behind him, driving five head of cattle.

"Look who I found along the road!" called Uncle Franklin, jumping out of the wagon to grab Aunt Ruthie and swing her around.

"Why, it's Ned!" they exclaimed, rushing to greet him.

"Hello, Ned," Suzannah said.

"'Lo, Suzannah. 'Lo, everyone!"

Ned was wearing a red flannel shirt, corduroy pants, high black boots, and a wide-brimmed black hat that didn't quite hide his red curls.

"Where's your pick, shovel, and wash pan?" Suzannah asked.

"In the wagon," Ned replied with a grin.

With his arm still around his wife, Uncle Franklin hugged Suzannah and Aunt Pearl. "How did our family get moved over to this side of the road?"

Aunt Ruthie started to explain about renting the cabins, but her blue eyes filled with tears. "The truth is . . . the truth is . . . Daniel's hurt. When you didn't get back right away, he went out for some supplies we needed, and someone hit him over the head and robbed him!"

"He's hurt?" Uncle Franklin asked. "Where is he? Let me see him!"

They tiptoed into the cabin where Daniel was sleeping on his side in Suzannah's bunk. When Uncle Franklin examined the back of his head, his face turned as white as Aunt Ruthie's had. He led the way out of the cabin.

Aunt Ruthie followed him. "He's been talking, but he can't remember much of what happened."

"Will he be all right?" Ned asked anxiously.

"In a few days, I expect," Uncle Franklin said. "He's young. It just pains me to think how much worse it could have been. It would be a hard thing to lose your only child."

Outside, he dropped onto a bench and buried his head in his hands. Then he folded his hands in prayer. When at last he looked up again, there was a peaceful expression on his face. "We're going to have to forgive whoever did this thing to him."

"Why?" Suzannah cried. "They hurt him!"

"I know," Uncle Franklin said quietly, "but the Lord expects us to forgive our enemies."

Suzannah thought of Charles. More than once, she had tried to forgive him for the trouble he'd caused ever since his marriage to Pauline. If only he'd changed his ways when she paid his gambling debts in Missouri, she thought bitterly.

While Aunt Pearl brought Uncle Franklin and Ned their supper, Uncle Karl sat down at the table with them. "I took it upon myself to rent you and Ruthie a cabin fer the month, along with one fer Pearl and me."

"A smart move," said Uncle Franklin. "It's getting too wet and dangerous to live outside now." Taking a sip of coffee, he turned to Ned. "Daniel will be glad to see you're with us again, son, when he wakes up."

"Took me a while longer than I thought to get back to you folks," Ned said. "I got too busy huntin' gold."

"Find much?" Uncle Karl asked.

Ned shook his head. "Not a whole lot yet."

"Same with us," Garth said. "We're doin' better runnin' this restaurant."

Ned seemed to be happy to see Suzannah, and she couldn't help smiling at him as she served thick slabs of apple pie.

When Big Red dropped by, Uncle Franklin introduced him to Ned.

"I've just rented out the last cabin," Big Red explained, "but you're welcome to bunk with me."

Suzannah was pleased that Ned would be living so close by until she heard Big Red's next words: "Yes, a good-sized family needed a place to stay. They'll be a mite crowded, but there was nothin' else I could do. You know 'em, since they came over in your wagon train—the Murphys."

*Oh, no!* Suzannah moaned silently. *Bridgette! Bridgette Murphy! It wouldn't be any time before she'd be batting her long black lashes at Ned again!*

The next afternoon, while they were washing the dinner dishes, the Murphys arrived with their oxen and two covered wagons.

"Hello, Ned!" Bridgette called over, looking prettier than ever in a violet calico dress the exact shade of her eyes.

"'Lo, Bridgette," Ned replied, turning bright red. Right before Suzannah's eyes, he seemed to grow taller just gawking at Bridgette.

"I'm ever so glad you're livin' here too, Ned," she said in her most musical voice. Then, noticing the pick he was carrying, she added, "Looks like you're goin' after gold these days."

"Yep, that's what I'm doin'." Ned shifted uneasily.

Suzannah was sorely tempted to dump her whole pan of dishwater over his head. "Come on," she told him, wiping her hands on the front of her dress. "I thought we were going to hunt gold around back."

He came to his senses. "I'm ready. See you later, Bridgette."

At least he hadn't completely lost his mind, Suzannah thought. "The miners who lived here were always picking and digging around these hills in back, and they got enough gold to go back East. Maybe they missed some."

"Could be," Ned said, falling into step with her.

The heavy rains had started a new stream in the back of the property, and Suzannah tipped back a boulder nearby. No gold. She tipped back another. None there, either.

Ned grinned. "Don't you believe in panning?"

"Never tried it," she admitted. "I'd rather just pick up gold nuggets."

He laughed. "Not much chance of that anymore. Everyone says the easy picking days are over."

He showed her how to swirl water and gravel in his pan, and she was just getting the hang of it when Charles cantered up on Lucky. "Heard you all moved here from across the road," he said as he rode by. "I brought another ham."

"Thank you," Suzannah managed. If he thought that stopping by with a ham every week or so was his only duty to Pauline and Jamie—

"Finding lots of gold?" he asked.

Suzannah just swirled the pan harder.

"Not here," Ned said.

"Where's Pauline?"

"In the middle cabin." Suzannah pointed. "We haven't seen you for a while." Charles didn't answer as he rode Lucky to the hitching post, so she called out, "I suppose you've been too busy gambling to come visit. Serves you right that you were robbed."

Charles pretended not to hear, but Ned gave her a strange look.

"Guess I didn't need to say that," she confessed. "It's just that Charles makes me so mad. He always brings trouble." She watched him dismount and tie Lucky's reins to the hitching post in front of the cabin.

"Gold brings trouble too," Ned remarked.

"What do you mean?"

"For one thing, I'm talkin' about all the no-accounts comin' to the gold fields now, like the ones who robbed Daniel."

"Desperadoes don't worry me much," Suzannah said.

She didn't want him to think that she was as helpless as Bridgette Murphy. "I can take care of myself."

"I thought you always depended on God to take care of you," he said. "You did on the trail. In fact, you're one of the people who taught me what I know about Him. Does this mean that you've given up on God?"

"Of course not," she said irritably. "Anyway, we're here now."

"Gold brings the fever, too." He gave her a curious look. "Lots of otherwise fine folks catch it."

"Well, I'm not one of them," Suzannah protested. All she wanted was to have enough gold so she and Pauline and the baby and Jamie would never again have to depend on Charles Herrington. Or was that just an excuse?

It was growing dark fast now, and a light rain began to fall. In moments, it was pounding so hard that the drops bounced off the rocks. They made a dash for her cabin.

Just as they neared the door, Charles hurried out into the downpour, holding a burlap sack over his fine hat.

"You leaving in this weather?" she yelled after him.

But he didn't answer her.

*Good riddance!* she thought and tugged open the cabin door.

The next instant she saw Pauline—gagged and tied in the barrel rocking chair—and Daniel tied to the bunk. "What happened?" she cried, then saw her trunk lid standing open and her clothes strewn across the floor. *Charles!* He had tied up Pauline and Daniel so he could escape with her gold!

She ran to Pauline and with trembling fingers tugged at her gag. "Pauline! Are you all right?"

If Charles caused her sister to lose her baby . . . or worse . . . she could *never* forgive him!

# CHAPTER
# TEN

In the lantern light, Pauline's face was twisted with pain.

"We have to untie them first!" Suzannah told Ned. She worked the gag off her sister's mouth.

"Get Aunt Ruthie and Aunt Pearl and hurry!" Pauline gasped.

"The baby?"

"Yes."

"I'll get them! I'll get them after I untie you!" Suzannah fumbled with the rope tied around her sister.

"Charles and I had words, and it almost . . . slipped . . . about your gold," Pauline said, heartsick. "And once he had a hint of it, he . . . he forced me to tell. When he shot the lock off your trunk, I tried to run out to get help, and that's why he tied us up—"

Suzannah swallowed, then helped her sister from the

barrel rocking chair to her bunk. "It's my own fault," she said. "I knew I shouldn't tell, but I couldn't help bragging. We'll worry about Charles later."

Ned had untied Daniel, and he sat up groggily. "Be careful," he warned. "Charles has a gun. He and his cohorts are the ones who robbed me. I remembered everything when I heard his voice."

"Charles robbed you and knocked you unconscious?"

Daniel nodded. "No question."

*I should have guessed it!* Suzannah thought. Seeing the ham on the table where Charles had left it, she felt like hitting him over his handsome head with it!

"Stay with Pauline, Daniel. I'll get Aunt Ruthie and Aunt Pearl!"

Suzannah and Ned rushed out into the rain with their lanterns. "See if you can catch Charles somehow," she told him. "I'll rouse everyone!"

As she reached Aunt Ruthie's log cabin, she heard a horse galloping down the road in the darkness. "I'm going to get you, Charles Herrington!" she yelled into the rain as she ran. "I'm going to get you if it's the last thing I do!"

At Aunt Ruthie's and Uncle Franklin's cabin, she hammered on the door and burst in. "Quick! Charles robbed us and tied up Pauline and Daniel." She turned to Aunt Ruthie. "Daniel's fine, but Pauline needs you right now!"

Aunt Ruthie came running. "Jamie's in my bed, Suzannah. Make sure Daniel gets into bed, too. And fetch Pearl!"

Suzannah ran to Aunt Pearl's cabin and told her the news.

No sooner had they stepped out the door than Ned raced up with his lantern. "Charles let the horses out of the corral! Must have driven 'em hard to get them movin' in such a heavy rain. But Big Red had his horse hitched up in front, and he took off after Charles."

Uncle Franklin ran toward the corral, Uncle Karl and Garth behind him. It wouldn't help, Suzannah thought. The horses would scatter through the foothills on a rainy night, and there'd be no finding Charles . . . and no finding her gold, either.

Daniel wobbled outside, holding a poncho over his head.

"Sounds like I'm your keeper," Suzannah said. "Nothing else I can do anyway." She had no horse to chase Charles, and she wouldn't be welcome while the baby was coming.

She checked on Jamie, who was just waking up in Aunt Ruthie's bunk, and argued Daniel into his. "I suppose I should tell you bedtime stories, but I'm so mad now I can't think of any."

"Story," Jamie begged. "Story!"

Suzannah groaned. "Me and my big mouth!"

"I'll tell you one, Jamie," Daniel offered as he lay down on his bunk. "Once upon a time there was a girl named Suzannah, who was so famous that folks named a song for her. She was also so exasperating," he said, grinning at Suzannah across the room, "that all they could say was 'Oh Suzannah!' And in California, the miners even made up some new words."

"Sing!" Jamie said, sitting up in Aunt Ruthie's bunk. "Sing, Daniel!"

Daniel grinned despite his pain, then croaked out:

> "Oh! Suzannah, now don't you cry for me,
> For I'm off to California,
> With a washbowl on my knee!"

He stopped, holding his head. "I'll sing more tomorrow," he promised Jamie. "My head hurts too much now."

"Thank goodness!" Suzannah said. She put another
log on the fire, then sat down in a barrel rocking chair. At
least Jamie and Daniel were in bed. If they talked all night,
she didn't care one bit. For that matter, she didn't intend
to close her eyes until the baby came—the baby that might
have *her* name.

After a while Ned came along with a lantern. "The
rain's let up a little. I thought we could go out and look for
the horses. Maybe they'll head back."

"Will you stay here with Jamie?" she asked Daniel.

Daniel nodded, then winced in pain. "Guess I don't
have any choice."

Suzannah pulled on a hooded poncho and grabbed a
lantern. Outside, she glanced back at her cabin, thinking of
Pauline and the baby. All she could see was a glow of light
around the rubber sheet draped over the windows. Charles
had probably caused the baby to come early. Oh, how
she'd like to wring his neck!

"Let's look in the corral across the road where you
used to camp," Ned suggested.

They slogged across the muddy road to their old
campground, then had to jump the stream and make their
way under dripping trees to the corral.

"Listen!" Ned said. "It sounds like the horses."

Sure enough, nickerings and whinnies were coming
from the corral. Suzannah held her lantern high and
looked into the circle of boulders. "They're all here . . .
under the trees!" she cried. "Charles probably couldn't
chase them much in the rain, and they ran right back to
their old home."

She laughed in surprise, but Ned said, "I prayed on
the way here . . . and you know what? I knew they'd be

here. I knew it! It was like hearing a still, small voice on the inside."

She remembered when she'd walked so closely with the Lord that she could hear that still, small voice, too. "So that's why you wanted to look here."

"Yep." He closed the corral gate.

The dripping of the trees filled the long silence, then finally she confessed, "I haven't prayed much for a long time, but . . . oh . . . I do thank God now. I've been as ornery and full of anger at Charles as can be. Just a few minutes ago, I'd have gladly wrung his neck!"

Looking up into the blackness, where a few brave stars were twinkling through the clouds, she prayed: "Oh, Lord, forgive me for putting gold and everything else before Thee. Please keep Uncle Franklin and Uncle Karl and Garth safe. And I thank Thee, Father, for letting Daniel live!

"And . . . heavenly Father, I do forgive Charles again. Give me Thy love for him. And . . . last, but most important, please let Pauline and the baby be all right. Oh, heavenly Father, I love my sister so. I couldn't bear for anything to happen to her! In Christ's powerful name I pray. Amen."

"Amen," Ned said. "Amen."

It was a moment before she could speak again. "I didn't realize I was praying out loud," she said, embarrassed. "The truth is, I held onto the Lord on the trail when everything was so hard, just like you told me. But as soon as I heard about the gold rush, that's all I could think about. I pretended I needed to find gold to help Pauline and Jamie and the baby, but it was more than that. It was like a . . . a sickness. No, it was really sin. I was putting gold before God!"

Ned spoke quietly. "Maybe Charles did you a favor by stealing your gold."

"Maybe. Anyhow, I don't care if I never see it again! And that's as true as true can be. One thing I've finally learned is that I have a problem with greed . . . and I don't plan to ever let it get the best of me again. I'm hanging onto Jesus instead."

"Whew!" said Ned, letting out his breath. "I was afraid you'd start acting like that Bridgette Murphy when you got older."

"How do you mean?"

"You know . . . flattery and fluttering lashes and thinking of nothing but herself."

Suzannah smiled. "Let's get back to the cabin. All I care about now is Pauline and the baby."

As they started back across the road, they heard voices. "Uncle Franklin?" she yelled. "Uncle Karl? Garth?"

"We're all here," Uncle Franklin called through the darkness. "But we couldn't find the horses."

"We've got them!" Suzannah said. "Ned prayed and the Lord led us right to them in their old corral. They're all safe!"

In the lantern light, she could see Uncle Franklin's grateful smile. "Guess He wanted the two of you to find them, because I've been praying, too."

A horse came pounding down the dark road. "Ho, there!" a man shouted. "You with the lanterns!"

"Big Red?"

"It's me," he answered, breathless. He reined in his horse. "Couldn't catch Charles. He'd already closed down his gambling tent in the gulch and ridden on. Don't doubt he'll spread a rumor that he was robbed so no one will suspect him."

"Sounds just like him," Suzannah said. "In fact, I wouldn't be surprised if we never saw him again. Come to think of it, I hope we don't! And I don't think Pauline would even care . . . not after what he did!"

They hurried across the road, slipping and sliding in the mud. *Lord, let Pauline and the baby be fine,* Suzannah prayed again. *Please take care of them!*

Big Red had ridden ahead, and now walked toward her. "Before you go in, I have to tell you somethin' in private. Come over under the restaurant awnin'."

Puzzled, Suzannah followed him with her lantern.

When no one else could hear, Big Red spoke in low tones. "I almost caught Charles. We were ridin' pretty fierce through the storm and mud, and his horse slipped, almost threw him. I grabbed for his poncho, but got hold of a burlap sack instead and nearly fell off my own horse. He rode on, never knowin' what I'd got from him. I figgered it was your sack—"

"My gold?"

He handed the sack to her. "Haven't looked. It's tied shut. I doubt any fell out."

Suzannah recognized the sack and felt the gold nuggets on the bottom. "It's mine all right, but not for long. I'm taking it to Uncle Franklin this very minute."

Big Red raised his brows. "That's up to you. I'll put my horse in the corral now."

Thanking him, she turned on her heel for Uncle Franklin's cabin. Once there, she scraped the mud from her boots and knocked on the door.

"I'm behind you," said Uncle Franklin, coming in from the corral.

"Stay with us for now, Suzannah. You're probably no more welcome in your cabin at the moment than I am."

When they stepped into the cabin, Daniel opened his eyes.

"Guess I should confess to both of you—" Suzannah began.

"Confess?" her uncle asked.

She handed the burlap sack to him. "It's full of gold nuggets I found by the backwater of the stream across the road. I never want to see it or any other gold again!"

Her uncle stared at her in amazement.

"I should have known better by now," she said. "All gold does for me is make me greedy . . . and takes my eyes off the Lord."

Daniel sat up in his bunk. "So that's why you've been acting so strangely."

"Let's just say I don't ever want to see that gold again!"

Uncle Franklin picked up the bag. "Feels like quite a lot of gold."

"I don't care! I don't want any of it! You're fair and good, and you can use it any way you want to."

"Maybe to buy a house in San Francisco?" he suggested.

She shrugged. "All I care about is Pauline and the baby." With that, she ran out the door and headed for her cabin. She felt lighter in her heart, as if she'd unloaded a mighty burden.

Stopping at the cabin door, she tapped lightly. "It's me, Suzannah. What . . . what's happening?"

"You can come in now, Aunt Suzannah," said Aunt Ruthie.

"*Aunt* Suzannah?"

Swallowing hard, she opened the door. She didn't remember anything about Jamie's birth, but she reminded herself that she loved him a lot, right from the beginning. But what if she didn't love this baby because of Charles? Or because of the danger to Pauline?

She tiptoed over to Pauline's bunk. *Oh, Lord, let her be all right*—

Pauline seemed to be sleeping, but after a moment,

she opened her eyes. They sparkled with joy. "Here she is, Suzannah . . . your little namesake, Anna. Annie, for now." She unfolded the top of the yellow blanket to show her the cozy bundle in her arms.

Suzannah gazed at the sweet pink face. Little Annie was sleeping as if she didn't have a worry in the world, her tiny fingers curled over the edge of her blanket. *She's as content as I'd be if I had always depended on the Lord,* Suzannah thought. Tears came into her eyes, and Pauline had to blink, too.

"She's beautiful," Suzannah whispered. "Really beautiful, just like you, Pauline."

Pauline shook her head. "More like you when you were newborn."

"Me?"

Pauline nodded. "I still remember."

Just then Annie fluttered her lashes and her blue eyes opened, looking straight at Suzannah.

Suddenly everything else faded away. Annie was such a new little person, and she wanted her to be happy . . . for God's love to shine through her to this sweet baby.

Her voice quivered, then she spoke from her heart. "Oh, little Annie . . . God's made you the very best part of this whole westward journey. And He's going to take care of us *all* the time now. I had to learn the hard way that we're not meant to live apart from Him."

Pauline smiled. "That's quite a sermon, Suzannah Colton."

Suzannah grinned. "Then guess I'd better end it like one: In Christ's powerful name," she added in her firmest tone. "Amen."

# EPILOGUE

At the end of November, the rains turned to snow, and nearly all the miners had left the foothills. Uncle Franklin and Big Red had just returned from San Francisco with a last wagonload of supplies for the few miners who planned to stay.

Uncle Franklin closed the cabin door behind them quickly to keep out the icy wind. "It's high time we go to San Francisco before we're snowed in," he said.

Suzannah was rocking little Annie in one of the barrel rockers. "We're beginning to feel settled in here," she objected, but not too strongly. The weather was so bad that they had to stay indoors much of the time now, and it was so cold in the cabin that they wore their coats and mufflers all day.

"We've found an old adobe house with two-foot thick walls on the outskirts of San Francisco," Big Red said. "It's roomy enough for all of you, and you wouldn't have to wear your coats and mufflers indoors."

"It'd be warmer for Annie—" Pauline said.

"How soon can we go?" Suzannah asked.

"Looks like the weather might clear tomorrow," Big Red replied. "I've already got some freezing miners lined up to rent these cabins as soon as we move out. I say 'we' since I plan to go along to help you with the move. You could be settled in the new house by Christmas."

Aunt Ruthie, Aunt Pearl, Uncle Karl, Garth, and Ned all spoke up for the move, and even little Annie gurgled in Suzannah's arms.

"Then let's go!" Suzannah said. "I don't want to be here in these gold fields another minute." By now, the whole family knew where she'd found her gold and had discovered more nuggets to add to the "house fund."

She handed little Annie to Pauline. "I'll start packing right now." An old adobe house with two-foot thick walls sounded like the very thing she'd yearned for for such a long time. It sounded like a forever and ever and ever *home*.

# *Go West With Daniel and Suzannah Colton!*

## Suzannah and the Secret Coins

When twelve-year-old Suzannah Colton is told to pack up her things to move West, the adventure has only just begun. On the National Road from Alexandria, Virginia to Independence, Missouri, she encounters bears, blizzards, and other dangers. But can she keep her secret coins hidden from her wicked brother-in-law, Charles?

## Daniel Colton Under Fire

Daniel Colton has just turned thirteen, and he's out to prove himself a man. But he's grown up in the city. Does he have what it takes to make it in the Wild West? A hunting accident, a near-drowning, and other wild adventures on the Oregon Trail test the limits of Daniel's courage.

## Suzannah Strikes Gold

When the Coltons arrive in California in the midst of the Gold Rush, Suzannah catches gold fever. But instead of helping the family, the gold she finds plunges the family into even more trouble.

## Daniel Colton Kidnapped

Life seems to return to normal when the Colton family buys a house near San Francisco. Then Daniel's father opens a most unusual store, and Charles begins to pressure Daniel to work for him secretly. Can Daniel untangle himself from the web of evil and deceit that threatens the whole family?

*Look for the Colton Cousins Adventures
at your local Christian bookstore.*